Kole Black

Autograph Page

The Chance She Took

THE CHANCE SHE TOOK

THERE ARE SOME CHANCES YOU JUST DON'T TAKE.

Written by KOLE BLACK

2 *The Chance She Took*

PREFACE

The Chance She Took is the story of Miss Rayqelle Davis, the stepdaughter of a Chicago police officer, who grows up in a seriously dysfunctional home and turns to the streets as a means of escape.

Broken and torn apart by physical and psychological abuse at the hands of her alcoholic mother, Rayqelle leaves the safety of the suburbs to live with her grandmother on Chicago's southside. There she quickly develops an insatiable fascination for the dangerous side of hood life.

That's when she meets Chance, an extremely handsome, very intelligent, hugely talented artist from a wealthy family, who turns her world upside down.

ACKNOWLEDGEMENTS

First and foremost I have to thank you YAHWEH, El-Shadai, Adonai, the God of Abraham, Isaac and Jacob, the God who created the universe, the sun, the moon and the stars! Alpha & Omega! You are the only true and living God! With out you, there is nothing, but with you all things are possible! Thank you for providing me the creative ability and affording me the opportunity to do what I was placed on this earth to do. I bow down before you, both now and forever!!! AMEN!

Now, I must thank every person that supported me in my dream and helped me along the way.

>*Sholina Penn*- You have been my joy and my pain, my sunshine and my rain! You cheered me on, when everybody else watched quietly from the sideline! You were there when nobody else was! I may have never finished this novel without you. So, now… I can't wait to cheer for you! "I'm waiting on> Broken". Get to writing!

>*Jeff "Jay's groove" Jones*- The insane genius. Thanks for the book cover design and technical support. If there is a way to do it, you get it done! You are the man who won't take no for an answer, the man who lives his dreams and the man who believes in the unbelievable. You are my brother! As long you are alive, I know that there is still at least one other dreamer left!

>*Anthony "Byiton" Washington*- 17 years of friendship! What can I say? Yo' tracks are slammin' and nobody slams 'em harder than you! You make me wanna' get my ass back in the studio! You are a truly great producer and songwriter! You are my brother for life!

>*Cathy Jenkins-McGee*- Girl, you are a dear friend, so many things have changed since "American Airlines" and so many things have remained the same. Thank you for being just a telephone call away.

God bless you and your family.

>*Sheila Miller*- my big cousin and the coldest woman of poetry in the Midwest!

Your "spoken word" is like "WHOA!!!" when the world gets a true taste of your talent; it will never, ever be the same!

>*Derrick "Graham Fay" Roberson*- You are one hell of a writer and Rapp producer! You've been a loyal friend and brother! Your die-hard creative approach is un-paralleled! You are a true visionary. Don't ever stop! Don't ever quit! There's only one "Graham Fay"

And last but not least! I would like to thank the editors at *Spaulden Publishing* for believing in me. Here's to the future!

This book is a work of fiction. All names, characters, places, and incidents are purely fictional. Any resemblance to any actual events, locales or persons, living or dead is coincidental.

All rights reserved, including the right to reproduce this book or portions thereof in any form whatsoever.

Copyright © 2007

Published by *Spaulden Publishing*, Woodbury, Connecticut, 06798

ISBN 978-0-6151-5348-3

THE CHANCE SHE TOOK

THERE ARE SOME CHANCES YOU JUST DON'T TAKE.

Written by *KOLE BLACK*

CHAPTER 1

Chance dashed down the last flight of stairs in the hotel with intense fear, the front of his clothes covered with blood, leaving crimson handprints smeared all along the wall and banister behind him. As he reached the bottom of the dimly lit stairwell, he quickly headed toward the back entrance and scrambled out of the huge, rusty steel door marked emergency exit. Chance could hardly catch his breath, so he stopped a moment and kneeled forward with sweat pouring from his face. He struggled to figure out what to do, where to go, who to call and how he got caught up in such a helluva' mess. As the sound of approaching sirens grew closer, Chance dipped back to the car, jumped in and pulled out of the dark parking garage. Speeding down a dark back alley, disappearing completely into the night, he was in complete shock.

Chance. It's a funny word, a strange word, and sometimes it's even a little bit scary. It can bring opportunity, adventure and even an element mystery. Lady-Bird used to tell me "Rayqelle, what you don't know, can hurt you worse than what you think you know." Ladybird was my mama, her real name was Brenda Dean but everybody called her Lady-Bird. She was an alcoholic and often spoke in riddles, so I didn't know what she meant at the time, but as it turned out, she was right. Ladybird was right about a lot of things. Which was kind of funny since Ladybird also used to tell me that I would never end up be nothin' but a lil' ho' or drug addict, a terrible thing to say to a little girl, but that's how she was. I didn't even know what a ho' was (but, I learned.)

I was born on the southside of Chicago, to Brenda "Ladybird" Dean and John Mitchell, he died when I was five years old. About a year later Ladybird married Jimmy Davis, a police officer who lived in Justice, Illinois, about twenty minutes from the southside. Then she got pregnant with Linn about a year later, I was the oldest. Well, me and my twin brother Johnny, who was killed by a hit and run driver when we were on our way home from school in the sixth grade. Ladybird never really got over it; she just tried to numb the pain with pills and alcohol. Officer Davis said, the day lil' Johnny died that Ladybird went with him. They just didn't bury her. Even though she still had me, Letah and Linn, she had pretty much given up on life.

I spent most of my teenage years breakin' just about every law I could think of, which was kinda' funny seeing as how my stepfather was a cop. I wanted to be good, but once I saw how being bad got me so much more attention; there was no turning back! I was always doin' things that I knew I had no business doin', always takin' chances that most girls would never take. I guess hopin' that one day maybe my stepfather might see how desperate I was for his attention. Though Officer Davis wasn't our real father, he was all we had. But it became clear that he really didn't have much interest in us. He worked really hard for the police department, so he wasn't home much and Officer Davis believed that a woman's place was in the home, so Lady-Bird stayed at home to take care of us, but after my brother died Lady-Bird started drinking a lot and was always in her own world, which pretty much left me and Letah take care of the house. This also included takin' care of my little sister Linn, who was born with congenital heart disease, so she stayed sick a lot.

Most of the time my stepfather would come home from work after a 12 or 14 hour shift, to find Ladybird passed out in the living room. Usually holdin' an empty bottle of vodka and he would just walk past her shakin' his head, but they never once argued, to be honest after Linn was born they barely even spoke. Really, Davis rarely spoke to any of us at all. He slept upstairs in the attic, we slept on the second floor and Ladybird would sleep down stairs in the living room, on the couch. She drank constantly to escape her demons; she said that it gave her comfort. Well, it might have given her comfort, but it made the rest of our lives a livin' hell! When she drank, it made her really mean!

When Ladybird was younger she use to sing. She even put out a record. My grandma said that she just about came out the womb singing. That's how she got the name Ladybird. But she gave up singing when she got pregnant with me and my twin brother. Which made her really bitter and she always managed to take out her bitterness on me. She never hugged me or showed me any kind of real affection and when nobody was around, sometimes she would slap me and tell me how much she hated me and how I ruined her life. She use to also say how ugly I was and how much I looked just like my black ass daddy.

Ladybird did a lot of crazy shit! She use to tell me that I killed her baby (my twin brother), and that it was my fault he got ran over and that it shoulda' been me that died instead of him. Later, as I started getting older she used to tell me that I would never be anything but a ho', because I would only play with boys. Or maybe she use to say that because she saw so much of her in me and that was the way she really felt about herself. Ladybird had gained a reputation when she was young for being the neighborhood ho', because she got pregnant so young. My grandmother used to tell Ladybird that guilt would kill her, if she didn't learn to forgive herself for the mistakes in her past and move on. But she never did.

As far back as I can remember, I only hung around boys, 'cuz I never trusted bitches! When I got older this eventually started rumors that I was fuckin' this nigga and that nigga, which was mostly a lie. I mean, don't get it twisted! I did whatever I wanted to do, with whoever I wanted to do it with, but I wasn't doin' half the shit people said I was. Most of the guys I kicked it wit' really were just friends. I never really had any female friends 'til I got to college, and even then the girls I hung wit' were more like partners in crime than anything else. I saw other women as the enemy! Maybe these feelings came from the fucked up relationship that I had wit' Ladybird, shit, I just figured that if I couldn't trust my own mama, I couldn't trust no bitch!

It seemed like the older I got, the worse my relationship got wit' Lady-Bird, 'cuz she was always on my back about one thing or another, always accusing me of something and always putting me down. So, I learned to stay away as much as possible. I never understood why she hated me so much.

Everybody always use to say how much I looked like her, maybe that was why she hated me, because when she looked at me she saw her own face and her own mistakes. Later on, after one of her many nervous breakdowns, she was finally diagnosed with paranoid schizophrenia, this mental illness that caused her to have hallucinations and made her think people were plottin' against her, mainly me for some reason. Which explained why she would accuse me of killing my brother (Who was run over by some fool speedin' down the street in a car) and why she even once accused me of havin' an affair with Davis. Apparently he had stopped wanting to have sex with her and as with everything else, I had to take the blame. I remember sitting in my room at night cryin', and prayin' to God that he would give me the magic cure to make Lady-Bird better, so she could love me. But, it never happened. Ladybird hung herself from a wood beam in my room the day before my fourteenth birthday. So not only did she kill herself, but she did it in my room, so that I would be the one who found her. I guess this was my final punishment for being born, her final gift to me. I had nightmares for months afterward! I never went back in that room again!

About then I started runnin' off to my grandmother's house on the southside, just to get some peace, just to get away. My stepfather eventually just let me stay with her. I guess he knew how much it hurt being in that house or maybe he was just happy that I was out of his hair and he really didn't have to deal with me that much anymore. After all, he wasn't my real father anyway. That's just how it always seemed. So, I resorted to the peace and quiet of my grandma's house. It was always quiet at grandma's, we all thought she hated noise, so nobody wanted to be over there but me, but I didn't realize 'til I got grown that she didn't hate noise, she just loved peace. I learned at an early age how to appreciate peace and the beauty of quiet, 'cuz Ladybird always kept up so much drama; I never really knew what peace was. Where my grandma lived was much different than where we lived, Davis called it "the no good hood." But I loved it, because everything seemed so alive, so loud and in yo' face.

As soon I got to the southside, it was like all my senses started to heighten. The sights, the sounds, and even the air, all overwhelmed me! Every little thing excited me. Which sort of helped me to escape the grief I felt over Ladybird's death.

My grandma lived right down the street from the South Side Shrimp Shack, you could actually smell the shrimp and chicken cookin' from her front porch. As soon as you crossed Western avenue, you could just feel the mood of the streets, you could see the hustlas' hustlin', the pimps pimpin' and the ho's hoin'. And sometimes you could actually even taste the filth as you walked through the streets, it was thick and real, it was so close you could smell it. The people were so interestin', so different from what I was used to, so alive. I got cool wit' a few people around the hood (the boys of course) who gave me my first true taste of hood life. Another reason I liked staying at my grandmother's was because she was really too old and too tired to keep up with me, so I kinda' did whatever I wanted. While she was busy cookin', cleanin' and runnin' back and forth to church prayer meetings, I was hangin' in the streets and acting grown (smokin' weed, drinkin' and talkin' shit wit' the niggas on the block). As long as I was back in the house by the time the streetlights came on, she didn't really trip. But, even when she did make me come in, I would just wait 'til she went to bed and sneak back out through the window in my room. Then it was really on!

Davis was cool with me staying at my grandma's, because he always knew where I was and what I was doin', or so he thought. What's funny is that he was supposed to be this great police detective but, half the time he never even knew what was goin' on with his own family or maybe he did and just didn't care. So many things went on with me right under his nose; he was just too busy to see.

My stepfather's emotional neglect eventually caused me to start actin' out. Ladybird was dead and I was starvin' for attention, but he was always so distant, which lead me to seek any kind of attention I could get, usually from boys for some reason. Which lead to me gettin' involved in sex at an early age. This was my way of satisfyin' my need for love that I wasn't gettin' at home. I had started to mistake sexual attention for love, only to be let down and disappointed. Then suddenly one day, it all made sense! I had discovered the power that sex gave me, and how it made men love me and wanna take care of me and made women hate me! Sex gave me a real since of control that I had never felt before. I had been going about it all-wrong! I started to see that I could have my way with any man. So I started playin' niggas and messin' wit' their heads. Sometimes I did it for money or material things and other times I would just do it out of spite, just to break a mutha' fucka's heart the way mine was braking. I used to call it gamin', and it was easy for me, because I had become so good at burying my feelings and doin' whatever I needed to do to get what I wanted. No matter who got hurt, as long as it wasn't me, I didn't give a fuck! I called it gamin' but deep down inside I was really still only lookin' for love, I just didn't know it. How strange it was to be lookin' for love and runnin' from it all at the same time. I was so confused. I was way too young, doin' way too much and usually my desire to be loved only led me into greater heartache!

CHAPTER 2

No matter how much dirt I did, Officer Davis always seemed to think I was this sweet, innocent little girl, but never quite good enough to be a daddy's girl. I had so many secrets! Like the time I got pregnant when I was sixteen, he never knew it, but I guess I can't blame him, 'cuz shit, he didn't even know when I got my first period. And as far as me being pregnant, I didn't even know. I just remember being really sick every morning for like a month, then one day I fainted and fell down the stairs at Grandma's, the next day I started having bad cramps and passin' these huge blood clots. (I was havin' a miscarriage.)

You see, while I was livin' with my grandmother I met this really cute guy named Monty that lived up the street. Monty was tall, light skinned, slim with a chiseled physique, light brown eyes and a big ass tattoo on his chest that said "MAKE MONEY", which was the name of the crew he ran wit'. He was fine as hell! I mean when this nigga walked by, the girl all paused! Monty was seventeen, had his own car (a BMW745) and mad paper to go along with it! And the boy could dress his ass off! He must have had every Nike jogging suit known to man. Monty and his brother Melvin sold dope, so all the lil' ho's around the hood wanted him, but he wanted me. At least for the moment anyway.

Monty's brother was one of the biggest dope boys on the southside, which was fucked up considering the fact that Monty's mother was a crackhead and everybody knew it. That's why they kept her in the house most of the time, to keep her out of trouble and to keep her from embarrassing them. After all how much respect would they get with their mother runnin' up and down the street givin' niggas head for a nickel-bump. So when she needed a fix, they fixed her. She was strung out bad too, if it wasn't for Monty and Melvin she woulda' been out there geekin' just like all the rest of the fiends. At first, I thought it was real fucked up that they would feed their own mother that poison. But, Monty explained it to me one day, he said that he knew she was sick and he just didn't want nobody takin' advantage of her.

Monty was very private about his home life, he only invited me into his house once and that was 'cuz I had to pee real, real bad! It was a real shit hole, it really should'a' been condemned along time ago! The paint on the outside of the house was pealing and the wooden steps leading to the front door were rotten and had some planks missing. When you walked in, it was dark, 'cuz Monty's mother kept the windows covered by heavy drapes, she had been inside so long that she couldn't stand the light. The air had the terrible stench of crack smoke residue and funky body odor. Monty's mother hadn't bathed in weeks and the spoiled garbage in the kitchen probably hadn't been taken out since the last time Monty's mama washed her ass! The place was so infested with roaches that you could actually smell 'em, it was a very peculiar odor, one that you would only know if you had lived in a place like it before. It was cold, dark and dirty, so I tried my best not to touch anything as I walked down the dark hallway that led from the entrance past the living room. When I finally made it to the bathroom, I just about threw up in my own mouth. A mass of roaches scattered everywhere when I flicked on the light. It smelled like piss and mildew from the sour wash rags that had been left laying in the window seal by the tub for days and there was a dead mouse laying right on side of the sink. Needless to say, I soon forgot about how badly I had to pee!

I couldn't believe how they were living! I was so heated! And so disappointed in Monty! Don't get me wrong, I wasn't mad at 'em for being poor, 'cuz that's something you can't always help, and I wasn't even mad at 'em for having mice and roaches, I have been places where people had both, shit, my grandma had 'em, but I knew the difference between that and this filthy shit! Monty and his brother shoulda' been ashamed of themselves, they both walked around with brand new clothes and shoes on everyday, but had the nastiest house I had ever seen before in my life. I was so disgusted and I knew I wasn't about to sit my ass down in that nasty bathroom. So I took a piece of toilet paper and politely pulled the handle on the toilet to make it flush, in case anybody was listening. Then I quickly got the fuck outta' there and tried to make my way through the foul odor of the living room, where Monty's mama and some dirty ass nigga were sitting on the couch looking like the living-dead, staring blankly at the television.

When I made it back to the car I didn't say one word to Monty, but he knew I was pissed and he was embarrassed. So that's when he started telling me that he was savin' up money to send his mama to a private treatment clinic in Indiana. It was supposed to be the best in the country. He said it was gonna cost about $50,000, and that was the real reason he was out here hustlin' so hard. I could see that it broke his heart, so I never mentioned it again. Monty loved his mama, no matter what she was and no matter where he was, if she paged him, he would drop whatever he was doin' and go runnin', "cuz she was an addict and there was no tellin' what might be goin' on, little did he know that my mama had been an addict too. We had more in common than he realized.

Being with Monty was like being with a superstar. Everywhere we went it was like everybody was watchin'. All the dope boys used to meet on Saturday nights at Giordano's Pizza place on the southside near the plaza. I was a little shy at first, being around all those rough ass niggas, but Monty used to say "Hold yo' head up, you my bitch!" and I did just that. I know it probably won't make much sense but, it made me feel sorta' special that somebody was finally payin' me some attention. You might even say that I was kinda' honored to be called his bitch, to be somethin' that anybody wanted to call their own made me feel good, that's how low my self-esteem was. This relationship would set the tone for just about every other relationship I'd every have.

Monty used to take me everywhere and buy me all kinds of stuff, the gamin' was easy. Most of the time I didn't even have to ask. Whatever he thought I wanted (Coach, Polo, Hilfiger, Nautica, Nike), whatever I wanted, I had it. But, he didn't even know that it wasn't about that, I was nothin' like those other girls he fucked wit'. I guess he thought he had to buy me, but I had another purpose. What he never knew is that I was so desperate be loved that I probably woulda' paid him to spend time wit' me. I didn't want anything from him, nor did I need it, all I wanted was his attention and the attention that being with him brought. I mean, my family wasn't rich but, I pretty much had anything I wanted and did anything that I wanted to do.

However, after a while I got used to the material things that came along wit' bein' Monty's girl and by then I was in love. But, not with Monty. I was just in love wit' the thrill of being wit' a hustla', the nigga that everybody wanted and the nigga that everybody hated. In fact being with him put me around some of the most serious hustlers on the southside, and he even gave me my first lesson in the dope game. I mean, sometimes I was right there watchin' him cook it, cut it, and serve it up, and nobody ever suspected that I was the step-daughter of a decorated police officer, if they had, I probably wouldn't be here today.

My family never even thought to ask who I was hangin' out wit' when I was at my grandma's. I'm sure they figured I had a little boyfriend at school or something, but nobody woulda' thought that he was this hustle-hard nigga from the southside, wit' a mouth fulla' gold teeth, who carried a nine in his waistband. After all what would somebody like me be doin' hangin' out wit' a nigga like Monty, a dangerous criminal from the hood, but the danger excited me! I was out of control and lovin' it! And I knew everything would be fine as long as I kept the hood girl separate from the good girl, which didn't seem to be a problem.

Monty thought the reason my daddy was never around was 'cuz he was a truck driver and was on the road all the time. I think that shit gave me some kinda' rush, I felt like a double agent. I mean, I was a "hot girl" when I was out in the streets with Monty and this "good girl" at home with my step-daddy (when he was there). My sisters never even knew what I was up to. Nobody did, 'cuz I kept my grades up in school and pretty much did what was expected of me at home. The whole thing was tripped out! Cuz, I wasn't even from the streets, I had just discovered the streets as a means of temporary escape from the shit I was goin' through with my family. Everybody was so wrapped up in being worried about Ladybird and my baby sister Letah that they never even noticed how I was changin'.

When I got with Monty I started dressin' different, actin' different, and talkin' different. Being around Monty and his brother opened up a whole 'nother world that I never knew existed, shit, I couldn't help but change. I saw alotta' ill shit first hand, like how mutha' fuckas would do anything fa'money. I got to see first hand how dope controlled people, niggas robbin', stealin' and killin', bitches trickin' and sellin' they food stamps while they kids sat at home hungry. Whole neighborhoods fulla' mutha' fuckas walkin' around like zombies, chasin' crack cocaine and heroin. Sometimes it turned my stomach and sometimes it turned me on. Monty and his brother used to say, "The hand that cooks

the rock, is the hand that rules the world."
They were right, but Monty and his brother
were not only involved in the dope game
but, they were major stick up kids too. They
would rob anybody, for anything, it didn't
matter if you were an old lady pushin' a
grocery cart or a young nigga pushin' a
Benz, if you had it and they wanted it, they
was gettin' it. They could be ruthless as
hell. I once watched Monty shoot a nigga in
the knee for bein' short $20 on some shit
Monty fronted him. What Monty wanted,
Monty got.

Monty always got what he wanted and
eventually he got tired of me, and Monty
got himself a new bitch. Which was for the
best, 'cuz about a month later him and his
brother Melvin ended up gettin' shot to
death by some niggas from Detroit that
they were tryin' to rob. The bitch he
dumped me for was killed by a stray bullet
in the crossfire. I guess Monty did me a
favor. That coulda' been my brains on the
concrete. He never even knew that we
almost had a baby together.

I was doin' anything not to have to be at
home. Since I wasn't kickin' wit' Monty no

more, I started spendin' alotta of my extra time at the library studyin' and readin', I guess that's one thing that probably saved me too. The strange thing was, that no matter how bad things got at home, I still always managed to keep my grades up. I remember Davis tellin' us if we got a good education that we could be anything we wanted to be and go anywhere we wanted to go. All I wanted was to get away from the memory of Ladybird.

So somewhere in between the streets and my books, I found my peace. After Ladybird died Davis did his best to make sure that me, Letah and Linn all went on to finish high school and then college. That was what he wanted, for us to go as far as our minds could take us. So I eventually made it through high school, I was so happy and excited about the future, thinking that somehow maybe my mama could see me and was finally proud of her little girl. No matter how far you go in life, there are some things that never stop following you.

CHAPTER 3

I met Chance about three years ago. I was a first year grad student studying psychology at Illinois State, I always wanted to help people and understand why they did the things that they did. Linn used to say I thought I was born to save the world and maybe she was right. Maybe I felt that since I couldn't save Ladybird, I had to help as many people like her as I could, to make up for it.

But anyway, Chance was an art major in his senior year. He had to be one of the finest guys on the whole campus. He was about 6'1, 185 pounds, smooth chocolate skin like a Hershey Bar, a slick baldhead like a milk dud, beautiful luscious, kissable lips, and a body that made you wanna slap somebody! He looked so good that I just wanted to bite him!

Chance was incredible; the boy spoke like four different languages (Spanish, French and two dialects of Chinese). Damn, I mean, how many black people do you know who speak Chinese? Shit, most of the niggas I ever met could barely speak english like they were supposed to, and on top of being well educated, Chance had to be the sweetest guy I had ever met. He would make candlelit dinners and take me on moonlight picnics. Chance knew just how to melt a ladies heart. He gave me flowers and candy, he even sang to me or at least he tried to (he couldn't carry a tune in a bucket.), but he loved me from his heart. He was every woman's dream, at least mine anyway. He was so quiet, so strong, so much of everything that I never thought I'd have. Chance wasn't from the hood, but he thrilled me in ways the hood never could!

From the day we met, Chance and I were closer than close, even more than inseparable, we were soul mates. Chance owned a beautiful home outside Chicago, in Lincoln Park, where he eventually asked me to come and live. I knew I had found the missing piece to my puzzle, my best friend, the breath of fresh air that I had been waiting for my whole life and nobody was gonna take that away! Please, don't get me wrong. Chance wasn't perfect, just perfect for me. He had his own share of issues just like any other man, but I felt really lucky to have him in my life. Cuz, where I came from a nigga either sold dope, stole cars or had some other kind of dumb ass, hair brained hustle that would eventually land him jail or in his grave. The typical thug ass, gym shoe hustler, stayin' caught up in all types of stupid ass drama (with the police, with other niggas, with they baby mama's, etc) and takin' you wit' him every step of the way. Those were the types of guys I was use to fuckin' wit'. But, Chance was nothing like that, he brought quiet to my life. He was like the calm at the end of a bad ass storm.

Chance came from a really good family, a very rich family! He was one of seven children, four boys and three girls. His father was a Harvard Law School grad, with a very success practice in Ohio and he was one of the first African-American representatives on city council where they lived. Chance's brothers and sisters were also doing well for themselves. He had a brother and a sister who were both lawyers, another brother who was a big time real estate developer, one sister was a police officer, the other brother owned his own trucking company, and his baby sister was still in college. We came from two totally different worlds but, Chance always let me know that it didn't matter where I came from; all that mattered was where I ended up.

Chance was a very talented artist; I used to love to watch him paint. My real father was an artist; he called it his great escape. I think one of the things that drew me closer to Chance was the passion that he showed for his work. He could spend hours painting and I could spend hours just watching him. Chance was always looking for different things to do to keep me excited. Not a day went by without him doing something sweet to make me smile. I gotta admit that it took some gettin' use to, I had to learn how to love and how to let somebody love me. I spent so much time running away from love, just living for myself, but never really loving myself. But, all that was behind now, for the first time in a long time, I was at peace, at peace with myself and at peace with being in love.

Everynight together was just like the first, and when Chance looked at me, I could see the love in his eyes. It was finally okay to let my guard down. I knew he loved me and it felt good! But I guess all good things are doomed to find their end.

>>>>>>>>>>>>>>>>>>>>>>>>>>>>>>>>>>>
>>>>>>>>>>>>>>>>>>>>>>>>>>

One night, Chance and I were out enjoying a beautiful evening at our favorite Italian restaurant, Angelica's on Michigan Ave. It was the third anniversary of our first date. It's also where Chance proposed to me last summer, it was a very special place that held some wonderful memories for us and this night was setting up to be just as wonderful! When out of nowhere two soft hands covered my eyes from behind, and a strangely familiar perfume lightly filled the air as a softly seductive female voice spoke.

"Rayqelle, Rayqelle. Never kiss, never tell." The voice said.

"I'd know that perfume anywhere! And that voice! Iesha? Oh my God. I can't believe it's you!" I said as I turned around in shock.

"Rayqelle Davis, you'd better get yo' lil' ass up out that seat and gimme a hug, girl!"

I quickly stood up and hugged the friend I hadn't seen in years. It was Iesha Ellis, my old college roommate and partner in crime. We hadn't seen each other since we graduated from UCLA and left California to attend grad school back here in Chicago, Iesha went off to New York to pursue her career in fashion design.

"Girl, you look too good! How you been? I heard you moved to Miami to work with some big name designer, or something. What brings you here to Chicago?" I asked as I hugged my girl again. I almost couldn't believe my eyes. Iesha was drop dead gorgeous, petite, only about 5'1 and 135 pounds, but supa' thick wit' it, and everything in the right place. Her skin was the color of honey, with a flawless complexion, her hair was a dark sandy brown with subtle hi-lights and her eyes were a deep hazel, like brand new soft suede. She wore a cream-colored two-piece Prada suit that fit her like a glove; her shoes were Prada originals with stiletto heels. This couldn't be the same ghetto ass bitch that I went to school with! I thought "Damn, did this girl hit the lottery, did she get married and kill her husband for the insurance money? What the fuck?" Anyway, whatever she was doin', she was doin' it well and she sure came the fuck up doin' it! 'Cuz she was nothin' like I remembered.

"Well, I'm here on business, visiting an important client." Iesha said shifting her eyes around the dark, crowded restaurant as though she was looking for someone she knew.

"Fashion related?" I asked.

"Not exactly, more public relations kind'a stuff. Ya' know." Iesha responded in a mildly evasive tone, with her eyes still glancing about.

"And how's your family? Letah and Linn and your step-dad, is he still with police force?" She asked.

"Everyone is fine, my dad's had some minor heart trouble, but nothing too serious though, he retired about two years ago and moved out to San Diego with Linn, so she could kinda' keep an eye on him. Letah moved to L.A. and... Oh no, how rude of me! Let me introduce you to my fiancé. Iesha Ellis, this is Evan Chance, the love of my life, and my future husband." I said proudly.

"Well, well, well, Rayqelle, Rayqelle. Girl, you always did know how to pick' em. It's a pleasure to meet you, Evan." Iesha said with a slightly flirtatious purr.

"It's very nice to meet you as well Miss Iesha and please, call me Chance." He said as he smiled slightly.

"Chance is a freelance artist and a very, very talented one might I add. He's one of the best in Chicago. Chance is working on the fine arts revitalization project for Cook County and he is also being featured at the Black Renaissance Gallery opening in two weeks." I explained.

"Oh, well, well, well, handsome and talented. Girl, you do know how to pick' em. So, when is the wedding? Have you two set a date yet?" Iesha inquired.

"Not yet, but soon, though." I responded.

"November 11ᵗʰ, this year." Chance said, which was a complete surprise to me since we had not even discussed a date.

"Girl, I guess y'all ain't wastin' no time, ain't that yo' birthday? That's so cute, congratulations!" Iesha said, as she hugged me and then Chance.

"Just don't wait too long. Some tramp might come along and steal him away, girl, he is fine and you know a good man is hard to find, and even harder to keep. I'm just kiddin' girl. Listen, I gotta get goin', my client just walked in. But here's my number at the hotel where I'm stayin', call me tomorrow so we can set up a time to meet for lunch and finish gettin' caught up. Chance, once again it's been a pleasure meeting you and I'll be lookin' for that wedding invitation. Rayqelle, girl, don't forget to call me. O.K.?" Iesha said as she quickly hugged me and hurried off to the other side of the dark restaurant, where she was greeted by a very handsome older man who kissed her on her cheek.

We both watched her from the table where we sat, it was clear that Chance was somewhat intrigued. You see, he was my man and I knew what he liked. I could see that he was attracted to Iesha, not in a way that disrespected me, but in all the subtlety that was Chance. He and I had a very unique relationship; it was different than anything that I had known before. If he saw a woman that he thought was sexy, he had no problem letting me know.

Again, he was never disrespectful, just honest. At first it made me a bit uncomfortable, but in a strange way I had come to respect his honesty. I ultimately learned to love him that much more, because he felt close enough to me to reveal this most personal part of himself. So much more refreshing than those niggas who swear that they would never even so much as look at another bitch, then wait 'til yo' back is turned to drool at every nasty little piece of ass that walks by. I felt safe with Chance because he was honest.

So, as we finished dinner, the conversation quickly turned to the topic of

Iesha. Chance was curious to why if Iesha and I were such good friends in college, I had never mentioned anything about her before. I explained to him that we had just lost touch and that so many other things had gone on since we graduated. She was busy workin' in New York, then back in Los Angeles, then Miami, then I had grad school to prepare for and to be perfectly honest I tried to keep in contact with Iesha for a while, but her ass kept movin'. Every three months the girl had a new address and phone number. So after a while I guess we just lost track of each other.

"Folks lose touch, shit, people get busy." I explained.

"And speakin' of gettin' busy, did y'all?" Chance asked playfully, with that devilish grin, that by itself could always get my panties wet.

"Did we what, Chance?" I asked, already knowing what he was trying to get at.

"You know, did y'all get busy?" Chance said, looking at me smirking.

"What? No, nasty! Now, why would you even ask me something like that anyway? You are such a freak, Chance. Iesha and I were roommates, and that's all! What do you wanna hear me say? Do you wanna hear that we kissed, we fucked, ate each other's pussies? Nigga, what? Is that what you wanna hear?" I quickly responded, as I grew slightly more agitated and horny at the same time, feeling my nipples start to harden. Chance's brashness excited me and he knew it. He knew exactly which buttons to push and what to say to get a rise out of me, and he did it everytime.

Chance leaned in close to me, smiled, licked his juicy lips and said. "Only if that's what happened and fa'real you really don't even have to tell me if you don't want to, cuz that was then and this is now but, I know a freak when I see one and yo' girl Iesha got FREAK written all over that ass. By the way, why are yo' nipples standing at attention?" Chance remarked, reaching toward me as if he intended to sneak a grab at my titty in the crowded restaurant.

"Boy shut up, you da' freak. You are nasty and you want everybody else to be nasty too! Come on here, pay the check and let's go. Dinner was great, now it's time for dessert." I said slapping his hand and standing up to head toward the door.

"Well, wait a minute, sit down. Why can't we have dessert here? They have Italian ice and that double chocolate cake with that whipped icing you like so much, and…"

" And what? Fool, if you don't get up and come on so we can go! Or must I spell it out? I'm ready for some dick! You know, the chocolate dick, with that cream fillin' I like so much? Let's go!" I was horny as hell and ready to go home and fuck, and to answer the question. Yes, Iesha and I did fuck around here and there on some freaky shit, but I wasn't about to tell him that, not yet anyway. Besides that, he wasn't ready to hear the whole story about me and Iesha and the part she played in my past, not yet, not tonight.

As Chance drove us home, I could tell that it was killing him not knowing what may or may not have happened between me and Iesha while we were roommates in college. But, he wasn't goin' to let me see how curious he really was and I wasn't about to tell him anything else. Because, as he said "that was then and this is now." And besides, tonight was all about us, and the mood was perfect. So I was not about let anything distract us from this evening's main-event, which was, me feelin' that long black dick inside me, all night. Although, I was gonna have to thank Iesha the next time we talked. You see, she didn't know it, but she really added some unexpected extra spice to dinner.

CHAPTER 4

So, on the way home I decided to relax and close my eyes for a moment. I guess I must have dozed off. Sometimes the night air does that to me, when I woke up we were at home, sitting in the driveway. Chance leaned back in the driver's seat with his pants already unzipped and open, his dick was standing straight up in the air, waitin' for me, callin' to me. Chance looked at me silently, but I knew exactly what he was thinking and what he wanted.

The light from the stereo glistened against the smooth head of his dick. It was fat, like the top of a wild mushroom, I wanted to put my mouth all over it and suck it, I wanted to feel it hit the back of my throat. I slowly reached over the armrest and touched him with only my fingertips as his precumm started to drip down the shaft of his huge cock. I took a deep breath and moved in for the kill. I gently placed my hands around his dick, stroking it up and down as I leaned over it, breathing him in and smelling the faint scent of his Calvin Klein cologne coming from his Sean John boxer briefs. I opened my mouth wide and swallowed his whole dick. Just then, I felt him reach between my legs and slid his fingers over my throbbing clit, into my already dripping wet pussy.

"Girl, where are yo' panties?" Chance asked.

Still slobbering desperately, I popped his big dick out of my mouth just long enough to answer, "I took' em off in the ladies room just before we left the restaurant." I immediately resumed my mouths pull on his fat black mushroom head. His moaning made my pussy wetter and his fingers inside of my hole was driving me insane. With all of the bobbing and sucking I was doing, I guess one of the buttons on my blouse must have popped off. Because before I knew it, Chance had one hand fingering my pussy and the other one squeezing my left nipple at the same time. He knew that shit drove me crazy. It felt so damn good; I was almost screaming, inside and out!

Chance moaned louder. I sucked his dick like the fate of the free world depended on it, I knew just how he liked it. He squeezed my titty tighter and gasped. "I'm cummin', there it is, I'm cummin'!" he said, as every muscle in his body tightened. He shot his cum into my mouth, buckin' and gaspin' for air, as I kept on sucking. What little cum I didn't swallow, came trickling out of the corner of my mouth, as he holla'd "aww shit! Yes!" I pulled my skirt up, and crawled over to his seat, "Give it to me!" he said, "You know what I want, gimme my dessert, I wanna taste you, baby please!" he begged.

So, I crawled up to the top of the seat, opened my legs over his face and settled in for the ride of my life. As soon as I sat down I could feel his long tongue slide up inside me. The feeling was so intense that I couldn't hold back, he was about to get what he had asked for. I was gonna cum right in his mouth. I rocked back and forth. His baldhead was wet with my juices. I reached back and felt his rock hard dick, I moved backward until I felt the head of his juicy cock pushing its way inside me.

I pulled his shirt up to touch his sweaty, muscular chest. Chance sucked my full, round breast as they hung down into his face; I grabbed his shiny baldhead as his stiff dick hit my G-spot over and over and over again. I got up and moved into the passenger seat and bent over on my knees. With out words, begging to be fucked. I wanted him to pound my pussy. I wanted him to fuck me speechless!

Chance got up from his seat and got behind me, spreading my legs as he stuck the head of his ten-inch dick between my pussy lips. He pushed it in long and hard, then longer and harder, then faster and deeper. I could smell the leather on the headrest as I leaned forward. The harder that he fucked me, the tighter I gripped the headrest. Before I knew it, I was biting into the leather as he fucked me. I gripped the seat so hard that my nails started breaking, one at a time, it hurt like hell, but pleasure of him far out weighed the pain of a few broken fingernails. Finally I could feel it, there it was, it was one of those "O's"! I mean the orgasm of a lifetime. I was exploding!

As his dick repeatedly hit my G-spot, Chance reached around and squeezed my nipples. I was goin' crazy! I felt like my heart was gonna burst, "Grab my hips and fuck me Chance, don't stop, I'm about to... there it is! Oh, yes! Yes! Yes! There it is!" I screamed. And there it was. I trembled from exhaustion as he held my hips, with his dick still deep inside me. I reached between my legs to touch the wetness of my own pussy. My body shook from the inside and my toes were curled so hard that my feet started crampin'! It was one of those "O's"! (The orgasm of all orgasms).

"Damn, yo' pussy is wet!" He said as he slowly started up again, strokin' me long and deep, then deeper, then longer and then little faster. Once again Chance grabbed my hips and dug in, I could feel him deep inside me, up by my navel. Faster and harder and deeper, then he clutched my waist as he screamed "I'm cummin', I'm cummin' again!" and shot his hot cum all over my ass and pussy. He pulled my hair to the side and kissed my neck. We both laid there for a moment, too exhausted to move or speak until the motion light from the house next door came on and shined into the car, sending us into a mad scramble for our clothes. Then a tired old voice spoke from just across the fence.

"Who's out there? What's goin' on? Chance, Rayqelle, is that you? Is everything O.K.?"

It was nosy ass Mrs. Thomas, the unofficial neighborhood watch commander. We hurried to fix our clothes as she moved toward the car with a flashlight in her hand. We both knew that if she caught us like this the whole neighborhood would hear about it by morning.

"Hi Mrs. Thomas, everything is fine, thanks for askin'. We hope to see you at the gallery opening next week, tell Mr. Thomas we said hi. Goodnight Mrs. Thomas." Chance quickly stuttered.

"O.K. I just came out to see what was goin' on, I heard some awfully strange noises, you kids be careful and have a goodnight." Mrs. Thomas said.

"Goodnight." We both said in unison.

As soon as she turned around, we both jumped out of the car and ran to the house laughing like two high school kids who just got busted makin' out in the park. Once inside, I slammed the door and I grabbed Chance by the hand leading him upstairs to the shower and quickly set the water. While unbuttoning his shirt, I kissed his chest and undid his pants. I could see his dick bulging through his shorts.

Chance unzipped my skirt, lifted my blouse over my head, and began to run his hands across my body. We hurried into the shower for a repeat performance of what just went down outside in the car. We made love under the steaming hot water for another fifteen minutes. We then stepped out of the shower and ran down the hall into bedroom, still dripping wet. We fell onto the bed with nothing between us but drops of water and the heat from our bodies, and passed out wrapped around each other.

CHAPTER 5

I woke up the next morning with Chance lying next to me, watching me as I slept. He had the strangest look on his face, as though he was almost mesmerized. He said that last night had to be about the hottest sexcapade that we ever had, and I had to agree! The passion over flowed from every angle. When I got out of bed he grabbed my hands and said, "You better go get those nails fixed, they're lookin' a little rough." And he laughed.

"Oh! Thanks for remindin' me. I need fifty dollars, and don't even give me that look. If yo' damn dick wasn't so big I'd still have my nails. So, cough it up Big Daddy. Never mind, I'll get it myself, I know where yo' wallet it is. And I need to get a few things from grocery store anyway, so, better make it an even hundred." I said rushing to beat Chance to the shower.

That evening as I had just returned home from the grocery store, the telephone rang. The caller I.D. said Chicago Hilton,

"Who could this be?" I thought to myself as I answered.

"Hello." I said moving about the kitchen, putting away the groceries.

"Hello, Miss Davis. I know you ain't forget to call me!" It was Iesha.

"Girl, I was just about to sit down and call you, I just got back in from the store. What's goin' on?" I asked excitedly.

"Well, I hope you don't mind, but I couldn't wait to talk to you, so I looked you up. Luckily it ain't that many Evan Chances in the phone book." Iesha said sarcastically.

I guess I forgot to give her my number at the restaurant. Anyway, we got to talkin' about old times and gettin' caught up on the latest gossip. Like, how this person was doing and who that person was doing, we use to girl talk for hours. Iesha told me that life in the world of high fashion wasn't all that it was cracked up to be, and actually she wasn't even really all that involved in it at the moment. She said, "Girl, listen, I had to make some hard choices. In New York City, you grow yo' ass up quick, fast, and in a hurry. I thought L.A. was tough. All I had to depend on was me, but I surprised myself. I realized that I had talents and abilities that I wasn't even aware of, like this amazin' power over men. I started to find that men just wanted to be around me and would pay alotta money for the privilege. I learned to do what I had to do to survive and even learned how to get rich doin' it."

Iesha and I both stood in an awkward pause for about 5 seconds. Then she said. "Well, girl don't just sit there and hold the damn phone. Are you still there? At least say somethin', please, hello…I knew I shouldn't have told you, I just thought you of all people might understand."

Finally, I responded. "Are you tellin' me that rich men are payin' you for yo' time and company, and conversation or are you really sayin' that they are payin' for the coochie? Cuz, either way you must be handin' out refunds left and right." We both laughed uncontrollably, the way we did when we were roommates in college.

I said, "Look girl, I ain't mad at you, at least you are gettin' paid. Shit, most bitches out here fuckin' for free, givin' the pussy to a nigga that oughta' be payin' for it anyway. At least you are smart enough to realize that ain't a damn thang free and if a mutha'fucka wanna play, he damn sho' gots to pay! Shit, I ain't about to sit up here and judge you, 'cuz we both know that I would be a hypocrit. I know you remember everything we use to get into, and games we use to run, so I would never judge you, but seriously, I just gotta ask, why. I thought you said that once you got'cho' degree, you were through with that shit, you said you would never go back to gamin' no matter what." I reminded her.

Iesha paused.

"Sure, I could go to work for some fortune 500 company, punchin' a clock, pretendin' to fit into their neat little corporate box, but I'm smarter than that, it's not me, it never has been and never will be. Plus, last year I made over $250,000." Iesha bragged.

I said "Damn, that's alotta' coochie."

"Girl, you ain't never lied!" She said as we laughed again.

"But that's enough about me for now. Tell me all about you and Mr. Chance, how did you land that sexy ass nigga? I know his ass gotta' be paid." Iesha asked curiously.

"Girl, why is everything with you always about money? It's not even about that with Chance. Look, I spent years running from love, gettin' wit' niggas cuz I thought they had this or that. Runnin' game on them, while they thought they were runnin' game on me. Yeah, sure Chance is doin' well as an artist and his family has money but, I got my own shit! I learned along time ago not to depend on nobody but me. Shit, fuckin' wit' Tico taught me that." I said. Tico Vega was my ex-boyfriend from college. He was a small time dope boy, wanna-be-pimp from Watts, who thought he was doin' big thangz. He was one of the biggest mistakes of my life and I have made some big mistakes!

"So, how did you meet Chance anyway?" Iesha asked.

"Well, I was with some friends at the Chicago Arts Invitational, one of their paintings was on exhibit. Chance was also being honored as one of Chicago's most talented new artists. He was fine as hell in that black tuxedo and I just had to meet his ass. One of the girls I was with just happened to know him from school, she introduced us, we hit it off and the rest, as they say is history." I explained.

"What? Girl, that had to be the first time in yo' life you ever took a chance." Iesha said jokingly.

"Well, how is it? Iesha asked.

"How is what?" I responded.

"Girl, don't make me jump through this damn phone and choke you! How is the sex? Is it good? He looks like he's gotta' big dick." Iesha asked. I knew it wouldn't take long for the freak to come back out.

"Well, you know I don't like braggin', but he is off the mutha'fuckin' chain, girl. I never would have guessed that a dick that big, went along with those little bitty ass size 8 shoes, and thank God he only got shorted on the feet. Cuz, I swear girl, the first time I went over to his house and got a good look at those tiny ass shoes, I swear I was about to turn around and go back home. I wasn't even about to waste my time. However, luckily nothin' could'a been farther from the truth, he had it goin' in every way that mattered!" I said unashamedly.

"Is he freaky? I mean, alotta' niggas got dick hangin' down to their knees, but don't know what the fuck to do with it! Just a damn waste of a big dick, in my opinion! Plus, if a nigga ain't got no tongue to go wit' the dick, I mean if he can't eat the pussy right, then he's already missin' 50 out of 100 points!" Iesha stated matter of factly.

"Girl, I see you ain't changed one bit, still just as nasty and nosy as ever." I said.

"Just makin' sure that nigga is handlin' his business, that's all. So, have you heard from Tico? You know he's supposed to get out this month, he wrote me askin' if I knew how to get in touch with you, talkin' about he's still in love with you and you gon' always be his woman. Talkin' about he was gettin' out and finna' get back in the game, and wanted us to come back to L.A. to help him get started. Girl, you know how Tico is, still on the same bullshit. He also wanted to know why you never wrote or came to see him. He also asked me if I thought you might have set him up to get busted." Iesha said pausing slightly, as if she was waiting for a response. I remained silent.

"Does Chance know anything about Tico?" She asked.

"No, I never told him none of that shit! I spent the last three years tryin' to put all that behind me. After everything went down the way it did and Tico got locked up, I just wanted to start over. I barely made it through college messin' around wit' that nigga, he had me doin' all kinds of fucked up shit that I knew I had no business doin'! Boostin', trickin', runnin' his dope all up and down the 405. That nigga ain't give a fuck about me! All he cared about was his money, 'cuz if he did care he never would'a... fuck it! I don't even wanna talk about it no more! Beside, I'm in love with Chance now and that's what's up, that's what's really good right there!" I said.

"Girl, Tico is a balla'! Tico gotz mad paper! Girl, Tico..." Iesha said.

"Bitch, Tico kicked my ass for two years! In case you forgot, I know I haven't! I'll never forget what that nigga put me through! I remember when he found out I was pregnant and made me have a fuckin' abortion! Then, I find out a week later that this nigga got another bitch pregnant at same time as I was. But he let that ho keep her baby, and made me get ridda' mine! And remember when he had his baby mama and her sisters jump me? Them ho's almost killed me, I was laid up in the hospital for like two weeks! Do you remember that shit? 'Cuz, I sure do!" I said.

I had to check Iesha's ass! 'Cuz she was known for trippin'. I had to put her back in her place right away and let her know that shit wit' Tico was dead! Iesha was cool but sometimes she had a way of fuckin' wit' me, I guess to see where my head was. Sometimes it was even as if she was tryin' to purposely get me mixed up into some bullshit. Iesha was a master manipulator; I had seen her operate too many times. So I had to let her know that I was not that same stupid little girl she met freshman year in college.

"Alright! Alright! Take it easy girl! You are just like a baby sister to me, I'm just tryin' to make sure that this new nigga is doin' you right. I admit it sounds like he might be holdin' it down, but it's hard to tell with you, cuz you're so closed mouthed and hush-hush about everything. I guess it's just that he seems so different than anybody I ever knew you to fuck wit' before. He's just so sweet, so quiet, so lame!" Iesha mumbled under her breath. "But in a sexy way." Iesha added.

"So, anyway girl. How the fuck did we go from talkin' about sex to talkin' about Tico Vega's sorry ass?" I asked.

"Well, since we are back on the subject, Chance must be the bomb. 'Cuz, damn girl, he got yo' ass sprung! He must got dat OUWEE goin' on! 'Cuz, you like, OUWEE!!!" Iesha exclaimed. She could so ignorant!

"If you are that curious, you should find out for yourself, I mean if you really wanna know." I couldn't believe what was coming out of my mouth and I'm sure that Iesha couldn't believe it either. But, I knew she wouldn't pass up the opportunity, I saw the way she looked at Chance. Plus, Iesha never could resist my seconds.

"So, what's up girl? You are a still a professional right?" I asked Iesha provokingly.

Iesha paused silently, "Girl, what you are askin' me? And bitch, yes, I am a still a professional by the way, even more so now than before, thank you very much! I even got a few other bitches on my team, kinda' like my own lil' agency." She boasted. Which explained a lot.

"So, what are you sayin', you wanna get paid, is that it? What? Because that's not a problem. How much do you charge for an evening?" I asked.

"I charge Two Thousand Dollars a night. This ain't that small time shit we used to do when we was workin' for Tico. I only deal with elite clientel, doctors, lawyers, athletes, politician, that kinda' shit!" Iesha responded. "However, for you, consider it my pre-wedding gift." She added. This made the hairs on back of my neck stand up, cuz this bitch never gave a mutha'fucka' shit without gettin' somethin' in return!

"You won't be disappointed and neither will Chance! You know how we do it." Iesha assured me with the greatest of self-confidence.

"Fine, tomorrow Chance and I have plans to go to that new club that just opened on the navy pier! Meet us at about ten o'clock, and we'll take it from there. I want this to be a night that he will never ever forget." I told her.

For a moment, I was speechless. Did I just invite my girl into a threesome wit' me and my fiancé? I guess I did. Chance and I had never done anything like this before, but we had joked about it from time to time. So, I guess it was time to put up or shut up.

Iesha and I said goodbye, and hung up the phone from what had turned into a three-hour conversation. By then, Chance was soundly asleep upstairs in our room. I watched for several minutes from outside the door as he slept, so peacefully. "Rest, my love. You're gonna' need your strength tomorrow, because I have a very special gift for you!" I thought, looking on as my chocolate lover slumbered unaware of the pleasure that awaited.

CHAPTER 6

When I woke up the next morning, my eyes still barely open and barely coherent, I reached across the bed to touch Chance as I always did, first thing, but to my surprise, he was already up. He was outside on the bedroom balcony waiting for me. He had prepared a beautiful breakfast of pork chops; eggs with cheese, blueberry pancakes and coffee made just like him, hot, black and strong.

I grabbed my robe and made my way out to the balcony.

"I must have been in a comma, why didn't you wake me? I would have helped with breakfast." I said, putting my arms around him to say good morning and also to thank him for the gorgeous spread.

"Well, I figured I'd let you sleep, you were on the phone quite a while last night. Who was it that you were talkin' to that late anyway, one of your sisters or something? Chance asked.

"No, it was Iesha. She said that she didn't want to take the chance of me forgettin' to call or losing her number, so, she looked us up. Who could forget about her crazy ass?" I said.

"Oh really, that was a pretty long conversation you two had. I'm sure it got pretty interesting, playin' catch up and all." Chance added playfully.

"We were just gossiping, girl-talk mostly. You know how it is when two old friends who haven't seen each other in a while start talkin', we just got carried away that's all. Chance, I wanted to ask you what you thought of Iesha. Did you find her attractive? I mean, you never really said anything other than callin' her a freak, but I caught you checkin' her out here and there. Did you think she was sexy? I wanna know." I asked non-chalantly while running my finger through the syrup on the side of the plate.

Chance paused briefly before cautiously responding. "Well, to be perfectly honest the two of you could almost past for sisters. You both have that same gorgeous ass honey brown complexion, almost the same height, similar features and almost the same sexy shape, and I mean, y'all both got ass fa'dayz! Yeah! She was fine as hell! Why all the questions about Iesha? What's the deal?" Chance inquired almost as if he knew that I was up to something.

"No reason, no reason at all. I gotta get ready to go; I have an eleven thirty class. Chance, please to come straight home tonight after your work out, remember we're supposed to go out to that new club on the navy pier. Thanks again for breakfast, baby. It was delicious. Gimme a kiss, I gotta go before I'm late." I said as I hurried off to get in the shower.

Chance walked slowly from the balcony and stood at the foot of the bed, almost puzzled.

CHAPTER 7

Later on, about two o'clock, as I was leaving class, my cell phone rang.

"Hello." I answered.

It was Iesha calling to make sure that everything was still on for tonight and that I hadn't chickened out.

"Don't be nervous, you are in expert hands. I assure you. Just relax. By the way, what are you doin' right now?" Iesha asked.

"Nothing much, just gettin' out of class. Why?" I asked her.

"Rayqelle, why don't you come meet me at Frederick's? They got a nice ass sale goin' on, maybe we could pick up a lil' something to wear for tonight. You know, to make it all the more interesting." Iesha responded.

"Alright, gimme twenty minutes and I'll meet you there." I told Iesha.

All the way there I kept thinking, "Is this right? Maybe, there's some shit you just don't mess around with. This was probably is one of them, because after all, Iesha was my girl and Chance was my man. What if something went wrong? But what could go wrong? I mean, we had never done this before and I was taking a huge risk, 'cuz Iesha could be a shiesty lil' bitch. What if she turned him out? What if they liked each other? What if? What if I'm just trippin'? Stop it, girl! Just stop already! It's just one night and it's just sex. Right? Of course it is! Then, why the hell am I sittin' here talkin' to myself? I am trippin'. Like Iesha said, I just need to relax. But I'm just gonna keep my wits about me in the process."

As I approached Frederick's, my cell phone rang again, this time it was Chance. He said that he had just called to see what I was doing and to see if I needed anything from the outlet mall, he was there picking up some art supplies. I told him that I was just out doing a little shopping with Iesha and that I would be home about seven o'clock. I asked Chance if he was still goin' to work out, he said "yes", and I reminded him to please home by eight, so that we could make it to the club in time. Again he asked what was goin' on and what was the big surprise. I told him to just trust me and that I would see him later tonight.

When I walked into the store, Iesha was standing in front of the main mirror at the center of the store, she had on a white boostier and panty set with the matching garter and stockings. Iesha was such an exhibitionist. The whole store watched as she strutted back and forth in an outfit that was carefully pieced together solely with seduction in mind. Iesha was really pretty, with a body like "WO!" 36-24-42. And she knew how to work it, because she had attention of everybody in the place, all eyes were on her and she knew it, including mine.

"Hey girl! So, what do you think? Will it make his mouth water? Is it too much, not enough, what? Gimme some kinda' feedback here, after all he is yo' man, and who would know better what to do to please him than you? Right?" Iesha said looking at me through the mirror's reflection.

"Yeah. He'll love it. I'll take the same outfit, in a soft baby blue! That's his favorite color." I said to the store clerk as she walked past and smiled bashfully.

"What's wrong?" Iesha asked as she turned around facing me.

"I'm fine. I just want to make sure that everything is perfect. I want this to be so good that he could live off the memories. Cuz, after tonight he's gonna have to." I told her.

"So, lemme get this straight! You think Chance ain't gon' ever touch another woman after tonight, just 'cuz y'all gettin' married? Don't tell me you livin' in that Grimm's Fairytale! Because I know plenty men who's wives live in that same fantasy world and try to make them live in it too, and most of them end up comin' to a bitch like me! Girl let me give you a good sound piece of advice, from one friend to another. Don't hold on too tight, you'll squeeze the love right out of him, and before you know it, well, you know the rest." Iesha said smugly as she turned and walked back into the dressing room, still commanding the attention of every eye in the store.

"Well, I'm gonna head on home and start gettin' ready for tonight, I guess I'll see you at the club around ten o'clock. Please, don't be late." I said as I soberly reflected on the reality of her last comment.

"Wild horses couldn't keep me away. And remember what I said. Not too tight." Iesha said stopping to look at me once again through the mirror with her back still turned as I stood behind her. I could feel her eyes watching me as I walked away, watching like a predator stalkin' her prey.

CHAPTER 8

As I got into the car, I started thinking about everything that me and Iesha did back in college, all the games we ran, all the niggas we played, all the foul ass shit we use to do for a dollar. I worked so hard to get away from that shit, to leave at all behind, and I'm a different person now, I've grown up, I just hope that Iesha has too.

I finally made it home around six that evening, in just enough time to finish up a few last minute details and I made it a special point to send Chance on a few small errands to keep him busy until about eight thirty. Then I thought maybe I would have a little drink to help settle my nerves, so I went over to the wet bar in the dining room and poured myself a double shot of Patron. I knew that I was gonna need all the liquid courage I could get, to make it through tonight. Don't get me wrong. God knows it's not like this is my first time gettin' down like this, it's just my first time with Chance, and as crazy as it might sound, I just want it be special.

By then about an hour or so had passed, with almost ninety minutes left, so I figured I would take a nice relaxing bubble bath. I had so many things goin' through my head as I slipped into the steaming hot water. Damn, it hit me! I was horny as hell and by the time that double shot of Patron finally kicked in I was feelin' pretty damn good. Hell, for real I was actually kind of looking forward to this little rendezvous. Had I turned into a freak? Shit, who was I foolin'? I had been a freak for years, but this will just be Chance's first time seeing this side of me, and only for tonight. Chance will be back soon. This was gonna be a night to remember. All my cares seemed to melt away as I soaked in the quiet of evening, hypnotized by the waters drip from the faucet, almost asleep I knotted forward and then I heard the door close down stairs. It was Chance. I could hear him as he hurried up the steps, calling to me. "Where you at, babe, you gettin'' ready?

"In here Chance. I'm just finishing my bath." I said.

"Rayqelle, have you seen my blue Tommy Hilfilger shirt? Chance asked.

"It's in the back closet, on the left hand side." I responded.

I watched Chance as he came into the bathroom to get ready; I could smell his masculine scent as he leaned over the side of the tub to kiss me. "Take those clothes off and get in." I said as my nipples hardened from the sight of his tall, slim, muscular physique.

As he sat down between my legs in the tub I slowly washed his body, taking my time as if we had no place to be. I moved the cloth over his big strong back, across his broad shoulders and then letting the water rain down over his smooth baldhead. I sucked the droplets of water from his neck.

"Don't start nothin' you ain't ready to finish." He said as he turned to look at me.

"You the one that ain't ready." I replied.

"What is that supposed to mean?" He asked.

"You'll find out soon enough, trust me." I said as I got up to get out of the tub.

"Where are you goin'?" He said as he reached for my hand.

"I'm gettin' out and so are you. Finish washin' up, Big Daddy, so we can go." I told him as the soapy water glistened over his body.

By then, that Patron was really starting to kick in and all my inhibitions were goin' out the window one by one. My heart pounded from excitement and anticipation as I watched Chance dress. Yeah, I was already horny as hell and I knew that in just a few short hours from now there would be no turning back. I wanted to grab him and strip his ass right back out of those clothes; it took every ounce of self-control that I had in side of me to hold back my hormones as they raged for him. And besides I couldn't wait to see Chance's face once me and Iesha got a hold of his ass. I couldn't wait to get back here!

Once we were both dressed and ready to go, I took one more quick survey of the house, making sure that everything was in place. Scented candles, slow music, and condoms placed inside the pillowcase, and chilled bottled water.

"Girl, let's go. How are you gonna rush me, then take yo' sweet time, and make us late? You better bring yo' self on!" Chance yelled from down stairs, while grabbing his jacket and keys. Everything was ready. So, Chance and I got into the car, and made our way to the club. It was only about fifteen minutes away, but that had to be the longest fifteen minutes of my life. The whole time I just kept thinking. "this is it, I hope everything works out like I planned."

CHAPTER 9

"This is supposed to be a really hot club! Everybody is talkin' about it and for forty bucks a head it better be the bomb. Oh and I hope you are ready to see some shit, cuz it's supposed to be off the hook up in there! When I say off the hook that's exactly what the fuck I mean. Jay said he came last week and it was a real live freak fest, girls on girls, mutha fuckas poppin' X and everything. So stay close to me" Chance said as we made our way down Michigan Avenue, toward the navy pier.

The parking lot by the pier was so packed that we barely found a space. As we got to the pier and approached the club, we could see that the line was a block and a half long. Chance was pissed, he said, "I don't care what they got goin' on in there, I ain't standin' in this long ass line! Forget it come on, let's go, we'll find something else to do tonight. Cuz this is ridiculous!"

"Let's just stand here for a while and see how fast the line moves. Please Chance. I really wanna go in and check it out! I've been thinkin' about it all day long, and if we stay I got a surprise for you." I whispered in his ear.

"There you go with that surprise shit again! What's this big surprise you keep on talkin' about anyway? What are you up to?" Chance asked.

"You'll see, just trust me! So, can we stay, please?" I pleaded giving him the sad puppy dog eyes.

"Alright, but we ain't waitin' in this damn line all night, I know that." Chance grumbled as he looked around at seemingly endless line people.

We couldn't have been in line more than five minutes when my cell phone rang. It was Iesha, "where y'all at?" She asked.

"In line at the club, at the back of the line, where are you?" I said.

"I'm inside standin' by the entrance, come on up front, I got us three VIP passes!" Iesha shouted into the phone almost busting my eardrum.

"What? Girl shut yo' mouth! Here we come now." I responded excitedly. If there was a hook up to found, Iesha would be the one to find it.

"Who was that?" Chance asked, as I grabbed his hand and quickly pulled him to the front of the line. Still unaware of the night that lay ahead, he follqwed like a lamb to slaughter.

"Just come on and follow me! Damn!" I demanded.

When we got to the entrance, Iesha was standing next to one of the bouncers, a big, black greasy lookin' nigga, wearing a tight ass silk shirt, that looked the buttons were about to pop off and put somebody's eye out! This nigga was sweatin' and breathin' all hard, and grinnin' at Iesha like he had just won a damn door prize. I mean, he was paying so much attention to Iesha that about ten people must have slipped right passed him and into the club.

"These are my friends Rayqelle and Chance, Y'all this is Big Rock." Iesha said as she gave me the secret wink.

"Come on in, y'all my guests tonight. Take these VIP passes and enjoy ya' selves. Miss Iesha, you gon' call me, right?" Said the big black ass bouncer as he salivated over Iesha's voluptuousness. Iesha smiled and winked, saying nothing, only running her fingers across his big sweaty chest as we made our way into the club.

"Girl, what was that all about? You know what, on second thought. Never mind, I don't even wanna know, that nigga smelled like he had cheese coneys under his arms. "Chance, you remember Iesha." I said as I watched the wheels turn in his head.

"Of course. How could I forget?" Chance replied charmingly.

"Girl, did you see that line? It was wrapped around the damn corner! And what was up wit'chu and that crazy lookin' nigga?" I asked, discreetly whispering into Iesha's ear.

"I was just standin' in line. He walked up and asked me who I was with and did I want some passes to the VIP. I said, "hell yeah!" Now here we are. Damn Chance you are lookin' tasty tonight, boy. You better watch out, somebody might take a bite' out cho' sexy ass! Anyway, I don't know what y'all came to do, but I came here get crunk! Let's go!" Iesha said as she grabbed my hand and pulled us to the VIP.

It was off the hook! The lights were right, the music was thumpin', and the drinks were strong as hell, but shit, I was already tipsy anyway, so you know it was about to go down. Chance could not keep his eyes off me and Iesha, and I could not keep my eyes off the both of them. Chance was lovin' it. Iesha grabbed Chance and took him out on the dance floor.

Chance was in awe; he didn't know what to do next. Iesha worked his ass on the dance floor and he kept looking back at me like he was expecting me to save him but, little did he know that I was one who set him up for the kill. They must have danced for forty-five minutes. It was weird watching my man being seduced by another woman, but in a strange way, it really turned me on.

While Chance and Iesha got their groove on, I made my way to the bathroom; my bladder was full as hell from all the drinks. When I opened the door, it was like a bad movie. Two bitches in one stall kissin', one bitch leanin' over the sink snortin' somethin'. Two other bitches in the corner poppin' somethin' in their mouths (x I guess) then kissin' and one lil' dark skinned bitch just standin' in the corner starin' like she knew me or like she was checkin' me out. It was some crazy shit. I mean, me and Iesha used to get buckwild but, I don't remember us gettin' like this. Or come to think of it, maybe we did, cuz we were doin' some of everything back then, and I do mean some of everything.

So. I pissed as fast as I could and got the fuck out of there, cuz you can't leave a bitch like Iesha by herself with your man for too long, cuz you'll come back to mutha'fucka that don't even remember who the fuck you are. Anyway, when I got back to the dance floor it was dark as hell and everywhere I looked it was like one freak show goin' on after another, like the shit that you see on late nite cable or girls gone wild (the ghetto edition). Guys and girls grindin', girls sitting in each other's laps tonguing each other down. I mean, it was people in the corner slow grindin' to fast music, mutha'fuckas walkin' around like zombies, the shit was insane.

Standing at the bar, tipsy as hell, I felt a hand touch the small of my back. I quickly turned around to see who was finna' get knocked the fuck out. It was the lil' chocolate chick that stared at me the whole time I was in the bathroom had followed me out, she was about 5 ft tall, she was cute as hell, and built like a brick shit house. I mean, she was sexy, almost as sexy as me.

"Are you here alone?" She asked.

"I'm here with my fiancé." I said pointing to Chance and Iesha on the dance floor.

"Oh really? Well, looks like he's got his hands full." She said as she smiled and started to dance closer and closer toward me. She put her arms around my waist and pressed her body against mine, as we moved to beat of the music.

"I'm Shela." She said speaking directly into my ear so as to be heard over the loud music.

"My name's Rayqelle" I responded, feeling slightly intrigued by this strange lil' piece of sexual chocolate that stood just inches away, offering her sweet temptation.

I could see Chance watching me as he danced with Iesha, never letting me out of his sight for more than a second or two. I knew he was watching, so I decided to give him a little pre-show. Shela and I dance, touching and caressing each other's bodies, looking at him, looking at me, looking at her. Shela leaned forward and pressed her full lips against me and I let her. I felt her tongue enter my mouth and I responded with the same. Everybody there had a role in the freak show. So, I decided to join them.

"I see you met Shela." Iesha said, dabbing the sweat from her chest with a cocktail napkin from the drink she held in her other hand.

"You two know each other?" I asked Iesha in surprise. Looking back and forth between her and Shela, thinking to myself, "Iesha, what the fuck are you upto now?"

"Shela is my personal assistant. She's here helpin' me with some P.R. stuff. Shela Simpson, this is my girl Rayqelle that I was tellin' you about, and her fiancé Chance. Shela didn't have any plans tonight, so I had her meet me here, I figured we could all hang out." Iesha said as she turned to look at me.

"Nice to meet you both, this is so weird." Shela said with the slight look of embarrassment.

"Enough talkin', let's dance!" Iesha said as grabbed Chance and pulled him into center of the dance floor.

So, we danced, all four of us enticing one another. When the song changed, we all moved to a corner table in the VIP, way off the side. It was dark. Chance sat down, and Iesha stood in front of him, giving him the lap dance of his life, as I sat next to Shela and watch. The drinks must have really started to have an effect on Iesha, because after that she leaned over and pressed her lips against me, as Chance sat and looked on in amazement. He was stunned, like a deer caught in the head lights, right then I knew it was time to take this little party back to the house.

CHAPTER 10

As the four of us made our way out of the club and to the parking lot, still laughing, dancing and havin' a great time, it was clear to all of us what was about to go down. So, I got into the car with Shela and Iesha, and Chance followed us in his car. Iesha was in no condition to drive, so I took the wheel. Iesha and Shela sat in the back. I watched them from the rear view mirror, as Iesha reached over and pulled Shela's dress down exposing her firm 36D tits. Shela moaned as Iesha began to suck her stiff nipples. Iesha moved her hand down between Shela's legs and I almost hit the car stopped at light in front of us. My clit started to swell as I sat at a stop sign with my fingers in my panties, watchin' these two bitches wild out in the back seat. Chance rode behind us unaware of the freaky scene that was taking place just ahead of him. Impatiently he beeped the horn!

Snapped back into focus by the sound of traffic passing by us, I stepped on the gas. I could barely keep my eyes on the road; the show in the rear view mirror was a dangerous distraction combined with the four double shots of patron that I had earlier. Shela and Iesha went at it like animals!

As we pulled into the driveway, I got out first, and then Iesha got out and came around to the driver's side and pushed me back up against the car. As we kissed, Chance got out and walked towards us. Shela grabbed Chance and kissed him on his neck. I watched them as Iesha fingered my very wet pussy. Chance looked on from the other side of the car, as our two silhouettes tangled in the dark night. Until, the porch light came on from next door, it was nosy ass Mrs. Thomas again.

"Who's out there? Chance, Rayqelle, is that you out there? Who's there?" she screamed from her window with a scratchy, sleepy tone.

"Who the fuck is that?" Iesha whispered in a startle.

"That's just the nosy ass old lady from next door, girl. Let's get inside." I said.

"Everything is fine Mrs. Thomas. Go back to bed." Chance said as he and Shela followed me and Iesha into the house.

Chance stood confused, almost dazed "Wait! Will somebody please tell me what the hell...?" as I lead him into the front door.

"Where can I get changed?" Iesha asked, looking at my man as like she was about to bite him.

"Rayqelle, what the...?" Chance tried to speak again.

"Baby, please just trust me! Stay right here until I call you, and don't move! " I said to Chance before I kissed him and I led Iesha and Shela up the stairs into the master bath where we quickly showered and hurried into the bedroom, while Chance disobediently eased his way up the stairwell.

I called to Chance as I set the music and lit the last candle. When he got upstairs the room was a glow, I reached out for his hand and led him over to the bed where I started to undress him, caressing his body as I did so. Once the last item of clothing was removed, I kissed his luscious lips, and laid him down on the bed, massaging his body with lavender oil. So lost in my touch, not even noticing Iesha on the love seat next to the bed eating Shela's pussy as she moaned in lustful heat.

Chance tried to speak. I once again pressed my fingers to his lips, as he turned to me about to ask the obvious question. But tonight there was no need for conversation, everything was clear. This night, with out any question was all for Chance and his pleasure alone.

Chance remained motionless while his eyes danced between me, Shela and Iesha. The three of us stood at the foot of the bed watching Chance, almost stalkin' him. Chance and Iesha locked eyes briefly as if they were the only two in the room. I leaned in closer to Chance, kissin' and biting his neck softly as Iesha moved to one side of the bed and Shela to the other. Chance watched Iesha out of the corner of his eye, in quiet disbelief, as all four of our shadows locked in a dance against the bedroom wall.

Chance and I kissed as Iesha's hands explored every inch of his dark chocolate physique. Iesha was visibly excited as Chance reached out firmly gripping her soft her honey colored body. She obviously got more than she bargained for with Chance and she apparently wasn't listening when I said, "don't let the small feet fool you!" Because when she pulled back the sheets, all she could say was "damn!", her eyes could have jumped out of her head.

Iesha was supposed to be the professional, but Chance had taken full control. I looked at Chance with the look that let him know that it was O.K. to lose himself, O.K. to jump in and get wet. So, I let go of his hand. This was my gift to him, a night of passion that he would never forget. And I couldn't believe it myself; I was actually sitting back watching one of my dearest friends fuck my fiancé.

As Iesha straddled Chance, sliding up and down, back and forth on him, I moved closer. It was as though I couldn't stop my self, almost as if they had a rope around my neck pulling me in. I kissed Chance deeply, while Shela took her turn and straddled his big black dick. I threw one leg across him so that I was facing Shela as she moaned loudly "God damn, yo' dick is in my guts!" Chance put his hands on my thick peanut butter thighs and pulled me over his face, licking and sucking me like I was the last piece of sweet potato pie at thanksgiving.

Iesha and I kissed each other as we switched positions. I could not believe my eyes, my lips or my hands. Chance buried his long tongue deep inside Iesha as she sat on his face; Shela got up as I took my rightful place on top of that big ass dick. Screaming "whose dick is this, whose is it? Tell me" I screamed. Iesha breathed deeply and moaned as her climax grew ever closer. She clutched my hand and told she was cumming, almost asking my permission. "Go ahead, girl! Let it out! Go ahead and cum!" I said. Just then Chance moved around and got behind Iesha.

"Remember that long black dick I was tellin' you about?" I reminded her.

Chance leaned over her and squeezed her titties, sliding the head of his big dick between her thick, wet pussy lips, teasing her every so slowly. Then, like out of no where, he plunged his big dick inside her like he had probably wanted to since the first time he laid eyes on her. There it was, I made his fantasy cum true. As he pounded her pussy from the back she started to scream, "goddamn, I'm cummin'! Fuck me, gimme that dick, give it to me, I'm cummin', oh yes!" Shela stood behind me, with hands on my waist.

Iesha's body quaked as she laid on her stomach, gasping for air. Chance moved toward me and stretched out his hands to feel my body in the dark, by this time all but one of the candles had blown out. Chance pulled me close and kissed me, I laid down on my back as he put my legs on his shoulders and pushed his long hard dick inside me. I moaned deeply as Iesha continued to pant, still worn out. Chance and I made love slowly and intimately, right next to Shela and Iesha as if they were a world away or not even there at all.

CHAPTER 11

With morning approaching, Sheila and Iesha got dressed and left. I put my robe on and walked them to the door and came back and watched Chance as he slept. That morning he woke up to find me outside on the bedroom balcony, patiently waiting for him. This time, his favorite breakfast was on the warmer with fresh juice and his favorite Chinese rose petal tea. Along with a single white rose.

Chance walked from the bedroom and sat on the edge of the balcony, leaning against the rail, reaching for me with one hand and reaching for the rose with other. He looked at me with a look that I had never seen, brushing the petals of the rose softly across my cheek, then without a word he put his arms around me, saying, "Last night was incredible, what made you do it?" I told him that I could see how attracted he was to Iesha from the very start and I thought that she might make a pleasing gift. He told me that last night was absolutely incredible and he thanked me, adding that it was the sweetest gift any woman had ever given him.

After watching Chance enjoy his breakfast, I immediately got myself dressed and headed out for the gym. As I drove down the road, the events from the previous night started to replay slowly in my head. I could picture every scene in vivid color almost as if I was living it again, the candles, the breeze through the window, and the smell of Chance's cologne coupled with Iesha's and Shela's perfume. For a matter of moments I was there again. Last night swept me away. It was even better than I thought it would be, especially with Shela as an unexpected addition.

Not knowing exactly how much time had passed, I arrived at the gym and never even realizing how I got there, but there I was in the parking lot of the sports club, cheeks flushed, nipples hard, and panties wet as hell! As got out of the car and made my way inside, I could still feel Chance's touch all over me. So, before I could even begin to concentrate on my work out, I was gonna need to cool the fuck off. Quickly I rushed to the locker room and got my clothes off, maybe the cold water would knock some sense into me.

Now, after taking the coldest shower of my life, I stood in the locker room dry off and still reminiscing on last night's freaky interlude. It made me question everything about myself, my judgment, my sexuality, and even my sanity. I just felt so relaxed and so comfortable. I guess I just felt as though I could let go of all my inhibitions and lose myself in the moment. Sure, I planned last night for Chance, but I enjoyed it too. It was a night that I would truly never forget.

There I was, standing alone in the quiet echo of the women's locker room, drying off and feeling the pleasure of my own touch at the same time. Almost allowing my mind to bring my body back to the place that required that cold shower to begin with. But a loud bang from a nearby closing locker quickly brought me back to a sober reality.

After my work out, I returned home to get changed for an afternoon appointment. I hurried through the front door, once inside and up the stairs I quickly moved to get undressed. But I couldn't help but stop for a moment to look at what remained of the night before. Everything left just as it was. The room seemed quiet and undisturbed. Chance had already left for an afternoon therapy session, so I was at home all-alone.

In the stillness of the room, I paused. Listening to the almost inaudible rotation of the ceiling fan in our bedroom, I was again transported back to the passionate calm of our intimate four-way encounter. Lying across the bed in the light of day with my eyes closed, the scent of Iesha's perfume faintly lingered along with the strangely pleasant memory of her lips against my body brought back old memories. For just a few immeasurable moments. All alone for just a few moments, in only the company of my memories. The afternoon's sun set high in the sky, casting a peculiar light against the same wall that had just held the shadows of four figures engaging one another in heated passion.

The light of day had an interesting way of making things clearer. When looking back, I guess the expression on Chance's face as it all went down was down, was all I need to see, and as I sat there quietly reflecting, all that mattered to me was Chance. Looking at the candles in each corner of the room, remembering how beautifully they shined against his chocolate skin last night.

CHAPTER 12

As I watched the leaves on the trees outside rustle calmly against the suns backdrop my cell phone rang. It was Iesha and the sound of her voice quickly snapped me back into reality.

"What's up, Girl? I just called to see what you were doin' today. Congressman Frank Jordan is havin' a barbecue at his house in Sky Vista and I was wonderin' if you might like to come as my guest." Iesha asked.

"Oh, for real? How do you know him?" I asked.

"Girl, I know everybody! He was the client I was meetin' the night I ran into you and Chance at the restaurant. Anyway, he asked me to come and he said I could bring a friend if I wanted. It's just gonna be alotta politicians and shit, and I just didn't wanna be there by myself, without anybody to talk to. He's gonna be pretty busy hob-nobbin' and schmoozin' for votes and contributions. So, I thought maybe you might like to go and keep me company." Iesha said.

"Alright Iesha I'll go, but don't be tryin' to get me caught up in one of yo' damn hoo-chee-rama, havin' that man thinkin' I'm for sale or no shit like that! Cuz, I ain't even on it! You hear me?" I said, making sure that Iesha understood me clearly. Iesha was also known for being a master of last minute surprises.

"Girl, quit trippin'. It's just a barbecue, and I would never even put you out there like that. What I do, is what I do and I would never put you in the middle of it. It's just a fundraiser for his new campaign and I just don't wanna be there with out anybody I know and who speaks my language. And it'll be fun and the food is gonna be the bomb! He is havin prime rib, lobster, shrimp and chicken." She said. Iesha was also greedy as hell!

"Alright, alright! I did have a class to go to this afternoon, but I guess I can skip it and Chance had therapy appointment to go to, that should keep him busy until I get back." I said.

"Therapy, what's wrong, he got a bad back or something, he seemed fine to me?" She asked.

"No, Chance slightly manic depressive, so he's on medication and goes to therapy twice a week to manage it. He's doin' fine though." I explained.

"Oh, hell naw! You mean that nigga's crazy?" Iesha said.

"No, Iesha, he is not crazy! Fool, he has a medical condition, and he is on medication to treat it! Maybe if yo' crazy ass went to see somebody about yo' issues, you could learn to stay in one place and quit bouncin' all over the country from pillar to post!" I snapped at Iesha.

"Well, excuse me for bein' concerned about yo' funny actin' ass! But, when they find you floatin' in Lake Michigan, all chopped up in little pieces, don't say I didn't warn you." Iesha responded.

"Look, wit' all the foul all shit you be doin', they'll find yo' ass floatin' long before they will me." I said.

"Anyway, girl. Where do you want me to meet you?" I asked Iesha.

"The address is 3514 Sky Vista Dr., pull into circle driveway, I'll be inside. Just come on in. I'll see you in about an hour." She said.

"Alright then, bye. As I said slamming my cell phone shut.

About an hour later I arrived, pulling into driveway in front of the house like she said. A valet approached, I felt just a little out of place handing him the keys to park my Toyota Camry, with all the Hummer's, Benz's and Jag's parked everywhere. I walked up to the big wooden door and before I could ring the bell, the maid opened the door. Iesha was standing off to the side, just behind her.

"Damn, girl. Finally! I thought you changed yo' mind about comin'. Let's go outside, I want you to meet the Congressman." Iesha said as she ran up and grab me by the hand.

I followed Iesha through the wave of snobby looks and turned up noses. The house was huge and beautifully decorated, and it seemed like we walked a damn country mile to get to the outside pool area where the Congressman was. The house amazing, like something you would see in Architectural Digest or some shit. I felt out of place, so I know Iesha's ghetto ass must'a felt like little orphan Annie or some shit.

So, as we stepped out on to the terrace the Congressman immediately spotted Iesha and motioned her over to where he stood. He was a very handsome, tall, well-built, light complected man, in his early forties, with smooth caramel colored skin and wavy salt and pepper hair. He had quite a reputation with the ladies. A most eligible bachelor and very, very wealthy.

"So, what the fuck is he doing with Iesha." I thought to myself. "I guess he must be slummin'."

"Hello my dear, havin' a good time?" the congressman asked as he greeted Iesha with a warm kiss on the cheek.

"Yes, Frank, I'm havin' a wonderful time, thank you. There's someone I'd like you meet. This is my old college roommate,

Rayqelle Davis. Rayqelle is a grad student at Illinois State study psychology." Iesha explained to the congressman in this fake, proper, wanna be boozhee ass tone that made me wanna throw the fuck up.

"Well, young ladies with brains and beauty seem to travel in pairs, Iesha is quite a young woman, in every sense of the word and any friend of hers is a friend of mine. Please, eat, drink, and enjoy yourselves. If you need anything, just yell for me. I have to go mingle, but we'll talk some later. Oh, by the way, Iesha. Did you get settled into your room alright?" The congressman asked.

"Yes Frank, I did, and thank you, for everything. I really mean it. " Iesha responded to the congressman.

"Good, I'll see you a little later. Rayqelle Again, it's nice to meet you and please make yourself at home." Said the congressman as he again kissed Iesha on the cheek and made his over to a small crowd of old moneybags, shaking hands and faking smiles at every turn.

I turned to Iesha with a look of utter amazement and curiosity. Iesha knew exactly what my next question was.

"Did you get settled? Into your room? Yo' room? You have a room? Here? In this mansion? What in the world did you do to that man, wit'cho ghetto ass? You got his old ass sprung! What kinda' game you runnin'? You know what, I don't even wanna know." I told Iesha.

"Wait a minute. Frank is a just good friend, a very good friend, I met him last year in Miami, and we have an understanding." Iesha said.

"And what might that be?" I asked.

"Frank wants to be near me, I understand that. So, I let him. It's that simple. and it's just until I find a place here in Chicago." Iesha said as she fixed her make up in the tiny compact mirror.

"It's just that simple, huh? I guess. Girl, you are too much. How did you manage to...? Never mind, I don't even wanna know, just be careful. You 'bouta have that nigga lookin for yo' ass wit' a flashlight in the daylight." I said with an even more curious eflection in my voice.

Iesha smiled with her head down.

"Let's get away from all these people. There's a beautiful aquatic garden down this way, come on." Iesha said as she walked toward the water garden, taking off her sandals. We stood at an obviously awkward silence, just listening to the tiny ripples over the rocks in the falls. Sometimes silence can speak louder than a thousand voices.

"Iesha, have you ever been in love? I mean, really in love. So much in love that you could see the sun rise and set in someone else's eyes. Have you ever met a man that makes you melt every time he walks into the room? Have you ever met a man that takes apart of you with him every time he leaves? Have you ever met a man that filled your heart with more love than you could possibly imagine?" I asked Iesha.

"Damn, look at you gettin' all mushy and shit. No Rayqelle, I haven't, but it doesn't mean that I don't want to. I'd give anything to have what you have with Chance, in a minute. I may never know that kind of love. You landed a really great guy and I can't say that'll ever happen for me." Iesha said as she watched the water flow against the rocks.

"Iesha girl, I think I may have landed more than just a great guy, I think I found my soul mate, and I thank God for him everyday. I mean, you know all the shit I've been through wit' niggas. I didn't think it was a good man out there to be found. Until now. But I had to change, I had to start lookin' at myself differently, I had to start seeing myself as more than just something to be bought or sold. I had to also stop only looking at what I could get out of a nigga, like if he didn't have this or that I wasn't fuckin' wit him. Cuz look at what that got me, I ended up wit' a nigga like Tico who flipped the script and sold me a fuckin' fairytale that turned into a nightmare. I'm just so glad I don't have to live like that no more." I said to Iesha.

"Yeah, I guess you have been blessed." Iesha said softly.

Well, what about the Congressman? It seems like he's crazy about you. What's that all about? I asked Iesha, even though I already knew what it was about. It was about money, just like it always was.

"Rayqelle I don't know, I don't know nothin' nomore. Sometimes I don't know whether I'm comin' or goin', leavin' or stayin'. I wish that I could find somebody who loves me for me, somebody that doesn't want anything more than just to love me. Ya' know? I watched the way Chance looked at you last night; the way he touched you was special. I laid there next to y'all, after he finished fuckin' me and listened with my eyes closed while he made love to you. He fucked me, but he made love to you. I would have given anything to be you at that moment. I mean, you have it all, a great career doin' what you love to do, a wonderful man that loves you. You've got it all and I have nothing. I don't know, maybe I'm gettin' really sick of sellin' my soul and my pussy to the one with the biggest bank roll." Iesha wept.

Iesha turned away and though I couldn't see her face, I could hear the tears in her voice as she spoke. She was my girl and I could feel her soul aching. Iesha hurried to dry her falling tears, as the sound of the Congressman's approaching footsteps against the gravel walkway grew nearer.

"Here you two are, I've been looking everywhere. Iesha, I want to introduce you to Senator Bob Tilson, he's an old friend of mine. I'm sorry, am I interrupting something? Are you two alright?" The congressman asked.

"Yeah honey, everything is fine. Let's go meet the Senator, Rayqelle are you comin'?" Iesha said as she looked into the tiny mirror on her compact to fix her make up.

"Yeah, I'll be along in a minute. I just wanna enjoy the water for a few more minutes. Is it alright?" I asked the Congressman.

"Of course Rayqelle, stay as long as you like. We'll be inside. Come along my love." The Congressman said as he and Iesha walked away hand in hand against the pink dusk of the sun. There was a strange calm, but underneath was great uncertainty.

As the festive get together came to a close, I politely thanked the Congressman for his hospitality, hugged Iesha and said I would talk to her soon. Looking back over my shoulder as I walked away, I could see Iesha watching me with every step I took, like a puppy looking through the window at the pound. It was the most sorrowful look I had ever on her face, almost longing; almost crying out for me not leave her or maybe wishing she could go in my place. I could see Iesha through the rear view mirror as I got in the car and drove away. I watched her stand in front of the house until I got too far away to see.

CHAPTER 13

All the way home I thought of how Iesha kept reminding me how great my life was and how lucky I was to have Chance. Yeah, I was truly lucky and didn't take it for granted for one moment, though I couldn't help but be just a little envious too. Iesha was still wild and free. She had no limits, it was all about her and there's a lot to be said for the ability to just be. It's a kind of freedom I'll probably never know again. And now she's living with a Congressman, in his mansion for God's sake. But at what cost? I wouldn't trade places for anything in the world. I could never go back to the life I use to live, not for all the money in the world.

As I arrived home and pulled into the driveway, I could see Chance through the window of his studio, quietly perched in front of his easel with brush in hand agonizing over each and every stroke. Chance painted the same way that he made love, deeply, passionately and brilliantly. The soft scent of jasmine drifted from the open window, along with the soothing sound of his favorite smooth jazz C.D., the one I bought him for his birthday last August.

Just watching Chance working, pouring his heart soul onto the canvas made my body weak all over. For the few minutes that I sat there, I imagined myself as his canvas, as he stroked me with long, deep strokes. I imagined him taking his time and covering every single inch of me with his color. Sitting anonymously in the dark of the driveway, I lifted my skirt, reaching in to my panties, sliding my fingers past the soft silk, to the waiting heat of my pulsating vagina.

Each time Chance moved his brush up and down, I followed his strokes with my fingertips pressed softly inside the wetness of my pussy. The longer I set in that car, the more I wanted and needed his actual touch. All of a sudden, just the sight of him was more than I could stand. He didn't know it, but he was about to be my chocolate nightcap, a much needed and very sweet ending to a very long day.

I walked in through the main door of the house, staring down the long, dark hallway at the ambient light peering out of Chances studio. I quietly got undressed at the door, dropping each piece one by one at the staircase. I tip toed lightly down toward the room that contained my dark stallion, the stallion that I was gonna ride all night.

As I approached the end of the hallway, all senses started to heighten. I could smell the hinted jasmine mixed with the aromatic fragrance of Chance's cologne, combined together with the sweet melody playing in the background, put me into a mild trans. My senses were totally over loaded by the thought of his hands on my body.

I was only a few steps away from ecstasy, so close that I could almost hear his heart beat from where I stood, just around the eve of the door. For a moment I stood captive, slowly turning toward the opening of the door, I caught a full glimpse of my tall dark lover, washed in the light that danced across big broad shoulders. There stood my prize.

The floor creaked as I moved forward, passing the jam of the door. Chance's dark brown eyes glided around to meet me. I was naked, more naked inside than I was on the outside. Transparent and completely open to anything he wanted or needed from me. Whatever he wanted, is what I was to be. All my inhibitions were gone. Chance moved toward me slowly and intently with the look that could only say one thing. He wanted me just as much as I wanted him. After making his way closer to me, he reached out, squeezing my breast, rolling my hard mocha colored nipples between his fingers. Leaning into kiss me with his full beautiful lips, he whispered, "What did I do to deserve this?"

And I answered. "Everything."

As he took his other hand and rubbed my thigh, traced along my hips, and squeezed my ass. Still kissin' me, but only much harder and deeper. Guiding me with his whole body, Chance maneuvered me over to the futon that he had setting directly in front of the window. The same window I watched him through just moments earlier, while playing in my own wetness, but now it was his turn to play in it, his turn to dip in to my juicy passion fruit.

We both stood in front of the futon by the window, touching and caressing each other with the desire of two animals in heat. He slid down to his knees, slowly kissin' and suckin' my nipples and licking my stomach. Biting me and tickling me with the lush, bushy hairs from his mustache. Slowly he moved from my stomach following the neat little trail of hair that led to my treasure.

Chance took his time, softly caressing the insides of my thighs, kissin' the top of my pussy, moving farther down, wrapping his tongue around my swollen clit and then sliding it in and out as he opened me up to expose all my wetness. Lifting my one leg up, so that my foot rested on the arm of the futon. Chance gently took his fingers and spread my juicy lips, and pushed his tongue as far inside of me as he could. I moaned and gripped his head as he explored me even deeper. With every lick that he took I moaned, softly at first, then louder.

"I'm finna' cum, suck it, oh yes, I'm cummin!"

I moaned aloud as I shot my pussies essence into his open mouth.

"Did you taste it? Was it good, babe?"

I asked as he stood to his feet, taking off his tank top and loose fitting jogging pants, exposing his long, hard dick. I fell back on to the futon with my legs open wide. The look on his face told me he was ready.

"Please, gimme some dick! You gotta fuck me! Now!"

Chance put his face between my legs; taking one more long lick from my ass to my clit and then back the other way again, almost sending me into cardiac arrest. My insides were screaming his name! He stood over me with his dick at attention, just looking for a moment, then he kneeled down and stuffed it into my mouth, and I dared not gag. Yes, he shoved his long, horse dick down my throat and I wasn't mad about it for a minute. This only served to make my pussy even wetter and ready for what I knew I had coming to me.

Chance laid on top of me and pressed his face against my titties, gently sucking and pulling on my hard, sensitive nipples as if he was gonna devour me. I could feel the head of his dick lodged against my pussy. Inch by inch he pushed his love inside, as I moaned deeply and dug my nails into his back. It was so big! It was almost too much for me, but I wanted it, I wanted him! As he moved in and out of me, I could hear the sweet sound of my juices flowing around the stiffness of his manhood. He pushed deeper, spilling my nectar on to the futon.

In and out, his long, chocolate nightstick plunged against my sugar walls and sent me into one of the strongest orgasms of my whole life, I could feel it in the depths of my soul. I was shaking all over. I never thought that there would ever be a man who could send me into a guaranteed orgasm each and everytime he fucked me, yet here he was.

After my epic explosion, I turned Chance around and sat him down on the futon; his dick was harder than a mutha'fucka'! So, I climbed on top and rode him like I was on a horse at the Kentucky Derby, and there it was. Chance clenched his teeth together and yelled "Rayqelle, I'm cummin', I'm cummin'!" So, I bounced on that dick even harder, until I could feel him squirt it all inside of me. It was warm and sweet. His body trembled in ecstasy as he leaned forward and laid his head against my breast, holding me tightly until we both drifted off into a deep, deep sleep and then the phone rang!

CHAPTER 14

The phone rang, once, then twice, then three times and then a fourth. The phone rang again, over and over again. It would stop and start right back up again. My grandma use to say "when a phone rings like that, it can't be nothin' but bad news." So, I reached and grabbed the phone off of the night stand, Chance jumped as I accidentally knocking the alarm clock on the floor.

"Hello! Who the hell...?" I answered angrily.

"Rayqelle, it's me Linn." It was my baby sister Linn and from the sound of her voice, I knew something was very wrong.

"Girl, what is it? Is Davis alright?" I asked with the sickest feelin' in the pit of my stomach as I got out of bed trying not to wake Chance.

"He's gone, Qelle. Daddy died in his sleep last night. His heart gave out." She said almost in a whisper.

I sat down in the chair next to the bed, knocked off my feet as the tears started to fall down my face. I began to weep, silently at first and then all at once it began to hurt too much to hold in. I dropped the phone as Chance got up and rushed over to me. "Baby, what's wrong?" he asked as he picked the phone up off of the floor. "Who is this? He asked.

"It's Linn, Chance. My dad died last night, he had a heart attack." Linn told Chance as I reached up toward the phone.

"Gimme the phone, lemme talk to my sister." I said. Chance handed me the phone and place his hand on my back to comfort me.

"It's me girl. I'll be on the first flight I can get! Have you talked to Letah? Does she know?" I asked.

"No, I can't tell her over the phone, you know how close she was to daddy. I'm just gon' tell her that he is sick again and she needs to come home." Linn said.

"Alright. I'll be there tonight. I'll call you from the airport when I get to San Diego. I love you." I said

"I love you too. See you when you get here." Linn responded.

I hung up the telephone and fell into Chance's arms while he held me close. I cried for another hour, and then I got myself together to go to San Diego and help make arrangements to bury my stepfather. Chance wanted to go with me ,but I told him that he needed to stay and prepare for his gallery opening. It was too important, and he had worked too hard and he needed to be there. I just told him to come in enough time for the funeral. Me and my sisters were gonna need to be alone anyway. Chance hesitantly agreed to meet me in San Diego in a few days and then he took me to the airport. This was gonna be the first time we had been apart since we met, but I had to go.

Later that night when I got to San Diego, I called Chance to let him know my flight had landed and that I would talk to him when I got to the house and got settled. When Letah and Linn got to the terminal to pick me up, I could tell just by looking at Letah that Linn had already told her. She sat in the front seat with a blank stare, looking straight ahead with her eyes were glazed over, but without tears. Linn said that Letah hadn't said a word since she told her and she didn't say anything the whole way home either. We all just sorta' sat quietly, letting our tears flow, feeling each other's pain. Officer Davis wasn't even my or Letah's real father but he was all we had and the pain in Linn's face was so evident.

As we arrived at the house, my cell-phone rang. "It must be Chance." I thought to myself. It was a Chicago area code, but I didn't recognize to number. I answered the call anyway. It was Iesha.

"Hey girl. I just heard the news. I called your house and Chance told about your dad. I'm so sorry. Are you aight? Is there anything I can do?" Iesha asked in her own sympathetic way.

"No. Just keep us in yo' prayers. That's all girl. I'm just so fucked up. I still can't believe it. He was fine and then..." I said still in shock.

"Yeah and I think it's real fucked up that Chance ain't wit'chu at a time like this. That shitty as hell!" Iesha said.

"What? No! He had to stay behind to prepare for the gallery opening. I told him to stay and just come out here in a few days for the funeral." I said, correcting Iesha.

"Yeah. Whatever! Anyway, I'm here if you need anything, aight? Do you want me to go by a check on Chance for you? Make sure he's eatin' and takin' his medication?" Iesha asked. Anytime Iesha offered to do anything for anybody out of the kindness of her stony little heart, I always got a cold chill.

"Naw girl. I'll just be gone a few days, then he's comin' right out here to be with me. Anyway, he'll be busy gettin' ready for the gallery openin', and his does not like to be bothered while he's workin'. He'll be fine." I said to Iesha, hoping that she got message to keep her high yellow ass away from my house while I'm gone. Not that I didn't appreciate the concern, but I just didn't trust her no farther that I could see her.

I hung up the phone and opened the trunk to get my bags out to take them into the house. As soon as I walked through the door, I heard a scream come from the kitchen. I dropped everything and quickly ran in to see what was going on. Letah was on her knees cryin' and screamin'; Linn was on the floor, clutching her chest, she was white as a sheet. I quickly called 911, and I tried to keep Linn conscious until the ambulance got there. She was struggling to breathe and sweatin' like a pig! When the paramedics arrived, they quickly got Linn stabilized and took her to the hospital. Letah insisted on riding with her in the ambulance, I drove Linn's car and met them there.

CHAPTER 15

When I got to the emergency room, Letah was talking to the nurse. She told us that they would have to run some test and it could be awhile before they knew anything. So I put my arms around Letah and we sat down in the waiting room. About an hour later the doctor came out and told that Linn had suffered a massive heart attack, but she was stable. The doctor also said the she was gonna need an emergency bypass, she had a collapse in one of her major arteries and that she might need a blood transfusion. He asked if we could both donate some of our blood just in case.

"Of course!" I said.

The nurse came out to take us to a room and draw our blood.

"Follow me please." Said the nurse. I walked behind her and was about halfway down the hall before I realized that Letah was still standing in the waiting room. I stopped and turned around.

"Just a moment please." I said to the nurse. I walked back down the hallway, Letah stood perfectly still as I approached.

"What? What are you doin'? The nurse is waitin', Linn is waitin'. What's the problem?" I asked.

"I can't." she said.

"You can't what? Girl, come on here and quit bein' a baby. I know you ain't still scared of needles. It'll be alright, you'll just feel a little pinch and that's it. Come on, do it for Linn." I said growing more frustrated.

"No! I can't!" She shouted.

"Why?" I asked. Letah turned away.

"I just can't! So, stop askin' me!" Letah shouted again.

"You selfish, little bitch! Our sister is layin' in that operatin' room, fightin' for her life and you can't, no, wait! You won't take a little needle stick? It's always about you, ain't it? You always have been a lil' self-centered heffa'! I don't believe you! This is so..." I said. Letah interrupted.

"She can't have my blood! I'm sick! Rayqelle!" Letah shouted!

"Sick how? What, you got a cold or somethin', what is it? We ain't got all day!" I demanded.

"Rayqelle, I am sick! I have HIV!" Letah shouted again as she broke down into tears.

"What? Oh my God, no, please God, no!" I said. "What? How? Why didn't you tell me?" I asked putting my arms around her.

"Please, time is of the essence!" The nurse said from down the hall, unaware of the serious conversion that was taking place.

"Miss Davis, please!" the nurse said again.

"I'll be right back!" I whispered, kissing Letah's forehead as I headed back down the brightly lit hallway with the nurse.

"It'll just be me." I told the nurse as she led me to the exam room. When I got back to the waiting room, Letah was asleep on the stiff vinyl love seat that was neatly situated across from the partitioned nurses station.

I sat down quietly, struggling not to wake my little sister as she slept so soundly.

CHAPTER 16

Letah was my baby. I remember when Ladybird and Davis brought her home from the hospital, and I held her in my arms and fed her. I use to rock her to sleep. She was so precious, she was my baby! Now to find out that she's HIV positive, I couldn't believe it, and Linn in that operating room about to have open-heart surgery and Davis was gone. "I just don't know what to do. I'm an emotional wreck. How do I move forward from here? How do pull myself together enough to be able to bury our father in just two days from now. How am I gonna get through this? Especially if Linn dies. I wont be able to do it but, I gotta be strong for Letah, she's gonna need me." I thought looking at her as she slept so peacefully.

Me and Letah sat in the waiting room while Linn was in surgery, it seemed like forever. One hour passed and then another and another. Seconds seemed like minutes and minutes like hours. Then finally a knock at the door, it was Dr. Bauer. He had been Linn's doctor since she moved to San

Diego, he was the best cardiologist in Southern California.

"Miss Davis, well we've done all we can and now it's...Well, all we can do is wait and pray for the best. We'll be moving your sister into recovery and the next twenty four hours are goin' to be the most critical!" Said Dr. Bauer.

"Well, can we see her?" I asked the doctor.

"Sure, she's heavily sedated though, so don't stay too long. What she needs more than anything is rest!" Said the doctor as he moved toward the door.

"I'll see you tomorrow, and try to get some rest yourselves." He added.

"Thank you, Dr. Bauer." I said softly, still sitting with Letah asleep on my lap as the doctor left the room and the door closed.

Quietly I prayed. "Dear Lord, it's me. I know it's been along time since you've heard from and I know I don't talk to you as often as I should but, I'm comin' to you now, Linn needs yo' strength, please touch her Lord and make well again, cuz we need her. And please Lord, just lay yo' hands on Letah, I know they say that ain't no cure for the disease she has but, it's in yo' hands.

About ten minutes went by and then I heard a knock at the door.

"Come in, it's open…" I said softly.

The door opened as a tall, broad figure entered the dimly lit room. I could not make out who it was, but then a deep voice spoke.

"Hey baby, I came as soon as I heard, come here, I'm gon' take care of you. Come give yo' nigga a hug and kiss, damn! I ain't seen you in over three years! Girl, you look good!" It was Tico Vega! The depth of his voice shook the room like the aftershock of a Southern California earthquake as I quietly trembled!

"What are you doin' here Tico?" I asked as my voice shuttered.

"I'm here to take care of my girl. I mean, you still my girl, right? "

Tico asked in a tone that demanded an answer of his liking.

"How did you find me?" I asked him, though I suspected I already knew the answer.

"I called Iesha to see if she knew how to get in touch with you and she told me where you was at." He said as he moved toward me, touching my cheek with back of his rough hand. Tico thought he was the shit! He was a tall, stocky built nigga' with an odd colored bronze skin. His father was Haitian and his mama was a full blood Mexican-Indian, which gave him a most unique appearance. His eyes were deep set and slanted, his lips were full, his nose was wide and prominent and his hair was thick, black and wavy. He was a light skinned, funny lookin' nigga', that kinda' put you in the mind of Max Julian, the man that played in -The Mack-. And that's just who he thought he was. He was really sort of ugly, but he had game like a mutha'fucka that more than made up for what he lacked in looks. I mean this nigga' could talk the funk off a skunk! It was just something about him that made all the bitches wanna say "yes!!!" to whatever the game he was runnin'. Believe me, I know what I'm talkin' about, because that's how he got me.

"Did Iesha also tell you that I was engaged?" I asked.

"Yeah, she told me about some lame ass nigga'. So what! You just needed something to tide over 'till I got out, I understand that but, Daddy's home now." Tico said as Letah started to wake up.

"My daddy is dead! And so is anything I ever felt for yo' sorry ass!" I said as my fear slowly turned to anger.

"What's up, Letah? Tico said touching her hair.

"Nigga don't touch me! What the fuck is he doin' here Rayqelle?" Letah shouted as she looked at me with confusion.

"Tico, you gotta go, I want you to leave, now!" I said as I tried to restrain myself from shouting in the hospital. The last thing these white people needed to see was a bunch'a niggas in here clownin'.

"Iesha said you needed me, baby. That's why I'm here." Tico said as he leaned in to try and kiss me.

"She lied! Now I want you to leave before I go get the police, Tico!" I shouted.

"The police? Oh, it's like dat' now? What? I ain't seen you in over three and this how you gon' do me? What? You think you better than me now, cuz you graduated from college and got'chu a lil' job? You think you better than me cuz you got some punk ass nigga wit a lil' money, payin' for the pussy!" Tico said as began to get angry.

"He ain't never had to pay for this pussy, you da' the only nigga that paid fa' dis!" I said as my anger intensified.

"Yeah, me and every mutha'fucka' you tricked wit', I pimped you bitch! Did you forget? I gave yo' pussy a purpose, you were nothin'! Bitch, I made you! I guess you forgot. You just a ho'! And I own you. I'm a real balla', a boss! You ain't shit without me! You better remember that!!" Tico said pointing his rusty finger in my face that smelled of stale Kool Filtered Kings, his cigarette of choice.

"Get the fuck out Tico!" Letah stood up and screamed as she snatched away from me and rushed toward him.

"Get back, bitch!" Tico said as he slapped her to the floor.

"Nigga you ain't shit, you ain't never been shit but a liar and a user!" Letah said as she grew more and more out of control.

"Yeah and I used yo' ass good, didn't I? I bet'cho you ain't tell Big Sis about that one." Tico said.

Letah lowered her head as if ashamed. "Oh, what? Don't get quiet on me now. Come on. You mean to tell me Rayqelle don't know?" Tico asked looking back and forth from me to Letah, grinning crookedly.

"Know what Tico?" I asked.

"About me and Letah." Tico said.

"What about you and Letah? I asked as my stomach tied itself in knots.

"When you left, as soon you left, this lil' bitch couldn't wait to get her mouth around my dick! You couldn't a been gone more than 24 hours before she had her lil' hot ass over at my house, fuckin' my brains out!" Tico said.

"Shut the fuck up Tico! I mean it!" Letah said leaping to her feet.

"What?" I asked in shock.

"I don't know what the fuck you gettin' all salty about. You wasn't givin' me no pussy anyway. After you got all high and mighty, started talkin' bout 'cho education and how you needed mo' out of life. You uppity bitch! But that's o.k. 'cuz lil' sis' stepped right on in and made up for the six months worth'a pussy you shorted me on. She gave it to me good too! Didn't you baby girl? And in return, I gave you your first taste of some real dick!" Tico smirked and laughed.

"What you gave me was HIV mutha'fucka! You gave me HIV!" Letah screamed at the top of her lungs as she started to weep.

We all stood in silence as the smirk on Tico's face quickly disappeared.

"Bitch, what the fuck you talkin' about? I ain't got no fuckin' HIV! You nasty ho, if you do got it, you ain't get that shit from me! Lil tramp, you lyin'! You was a ho' anyway. You was fuckin'' yo' own daddy!" Tico said shaking his head in stunned disbelief.

"I loved you!" Letah sobbed as tears streamed down her face and I began to tremble.

"You told me you loved me and that you loved me from the first time we met!" Letah added through a mass of tears.

"Lyin' ass bitch! I ain't never tell I loved you! You was just some pussy to hold me over 'til some real shit came along. Besides, I was just lettin' you hide out from yo' crazy ass daddy, 'cuz he was molestin' yo ass! Oh what? Don't tell me she don't know that shit either?" He said as he looked back and forth between me and Letah. Tico laughed arrogantly.

"Shut the fuck up, Tico!" Letah shouted.

"What? What is he talking about? Did something happen? Did Davis do something to you?" I asked as stood stunned.

Letah cried. "He said if I told that he would make something happen to you and Linn! He said that he needed me. He said that if I told, that nobody would believe me 'cuz he was a police officer. When Ladybird found out, she blamed herself. "

I threw my hand up into the air and interrupted her. "What, are you saying? Are you telling me that Ladybird knew that Davis was hurting you? And she didn't do anything about it? Is that what you are tellin' me?" I asked in disbelief, as I grabbed Letah by the shoulders.

"I heard them argue. She told Davis that she was taking us and leaving. Davis said that everybody knew that she was crazy and nobody was gonna believe her. He said that if she told he would have her locked up forever and she would never see her children again. That was two days before yo' fourteenth birthday. The next day she was dead, she had hung herself. Everybody was just going through so much, so, I never told. But after you left to go back to Chicago for grad school, Tico called and told me all this shit about how much he loved me and that it was me he always wanted. And I told him about Davis and he said that he would protect me and that he wanted me to come stay with him. So I stayed there for a few months, really just to get away from Davis, but Tico just wanted to pimp me, so I ran away from him too. Then I was going to join the army to get away from town and try to make something of myself. When I went for my physical I found out that I was HIV positive." She struggled to speak through a waterfall of tears.

"This bitch is lyin' to you baby, I ain't sick, come on baby. Look at me. Do I look sick? " Tico said to me as he reached out to touched my hand.

"You don't have to look sick to have HIV, you stupid mutha'fucka... Oh no! Oh no! You mean to tell I might have HIV? I just got tested last year. I gotta' get tested! What about Chance? Oh my god! And I just shared me blood with Linn. I need to find out if they gave her any of my blood! Oh, God! I said as I stormed out of the door passed Tico. He grabbed at my arm, but I yanked away.

"You gon' get yours, nigga, I swear on everything I love!" Letah shouted to Tico as he quickly walked out of the door following behind me, leaving her still sobbing.

I ran and found Linn's doctor right away to make sure that she hadn't received any of the blood they took from me. I explained the situation to him, telling him that might have been infected and I needed to be tested immediately. He set up the tests right away, luckily there was a lab on site at the hospital. They were able to run some kind of rapid test that came back in 4 hours.

And the clock began to tick!

CHAPTER 17

The wait was pure torture! I sat in the waiting room with Letah. She kept apologizing and trying to explain, but I didn't even wanna hear it. All I could think about was Linn and Chance. And the frustrating part was that I didn't even wanna tell him until I knew something, one way or another. He called several times while I was waiting on the results, but I just kept sending him to my voicemail. I couldn't talk to him yet. What if I had infected him with this virus? What if? Oh my God! What about Iesha and her friend Sheila? We had just had that threesome. "Oh God please!" I begged.

Then the nurse came around the corner.

"I have the results of your test." She said as the terror caused my heart to stop beating for just a moment.

"It was negative for HIV, but because there is possibility that you have been exposed to the virus, you'll need to get tested again in six months." She said as I sighed in relief and breathed again.

"Thank you, Jesus!!!" I shouted out loud.

Letah stood quietly looking out into space. I wanted to slap the shit outta' her ass for betraying me, but there were too many other things going on that we needed to get through.

Linn was still in intensive care and we still had Davis's funeral to prepare for. So, after we went and looked in on Linn, Letah and I headed back to the house to get unpacked and to start making the arrangements for our stepfather's burial. As it turns out, Letah was infected before she even started messing around with Tico, and Davis had to be the one who infected her, after years of having countless unprotected sexual encounters with prostitutes. It was all too deep and too sorted and I wanted to discuss it, but I was way too tired! I was on the verge of a nervous break down and it was all I could do just to get us home without wrecking the car.

The ride home was dead quiet and once we got back to the house, I just wanted to lay down and try to close my eyes for a few hours. So, I drug myself upstairs to one of the spare bedrooms, got undressed and fell into bed. When I turned the lights out, I could see Letah's silhouette standing in the doorway. She looked just like a little kid, the way she use to stand outside my room at night when she was scared.

"Come on in here." I said softly, just like I use to when she was a kid. Letah entered the room with out a word and just laid herself down beside me and put her head against my shoulder. We were still sisters and that night we both struggled to sleep, with what seemed like the weight of the world heavy on both our hearts.

The next morning, I was awakened by the sound of a ringtone playing me and Chance's favorite song on my cell-phone (Mary J. Blige, Can't be without you.) It was Chance. He said he had been trying to get through all night. He wanted to know how everything was going. He said that he missed me and wanted to know why I hadn't called. I told him that with everything that was going on, I hadn't had time. I wanted to tell him about what happened with Tico so badly, but I knew better, and I wanted to tell him what I had learned about Davis. But, if Chance had any idea what the fuck was going on here, he would be on a plane faster than I could even finish telling him. I also knew that this would be a real fucked up way for him find out about my past. So, I decided to wait. Even though I knew there would never be good time to tell him, I just knew that the time wasn't right now. I had enough shit to deal with!

Chance asked if I had talked to Iesha, he said that she stopped by a few time already, ringing the doorbell, but he said that he didn't answer. He never answered the door, even if I was there. He wasn't really much of a people person anyway and really didn't like to be bothered. He just wanted to know why she would keep coming by knowing that I was away. I had a pretty good idea about why, I'm just glad he didn't open that door. There's no telling what that skank was upto.

Chance said that he was just about ready for the gallery opening and that he had been driving himself crazy thinking about me. It was so nice to hear his voice. I guess I didn't realize how much I would miss him either, but it was really hard to think of anything except this mess with Davis. I told Chance that I still had to go down stairs to his room and pick out a suit to bury him in and then take it over to the funeral home. Chance said that he would be here tomorrow night about eleven o'clock. I could not wait! I needed my man to hold me.

Just then the other line on the phone beeped in, it was the hospital. I quickly told Chance that I loved him and I'd call him back later.

It was Linn's doctor, he said that she was doing better, but couldn't be moved from the I.C.U. for another few days, that would mean that she'd miss her father's funeral. He said that there was no way she would be able to make it. He said that we could come visit, but only briefly, because she still needed her rest. I thanked the doctor for everything and got off the phone.

Just then, the doorbell rang, Letah answered and yelled up the stairs for me to come down to the door. It was a police detective from the San Diego County

Sheriff's department, he said he had come by to ask Linn a few questions about Davis's death. He said that the toxicology report from the autopsy showed a high level of arsenic that suggested he had been poisoned, either accidentally or on purpose. I explained to him that Linn was in the hospital in intensive care and we didn't know when she would be home.

The detective had a team of crime scene investigators waiting outside with a warrant to come in and search the premises. They came in, looked around for about an hour, put a few things in some bags and boxes and left. The detective said that he would be in touch. I stood puzzled.

"Why would Linn wanna kill her own father? There had to be some logical explanation for all this shit!" I thought.

Letah sat quietly on the sofa, gazing into the ashes of the empty fireplace.

The next day Chance's flight was delayed so he arrived to the house just as we were leaving for the funeral. He parked his car and jumped into the limousine with me and Letah. We got to the funeral home at about 11 o'clock that morning and Linn was still in intensive care. The funeral home looked like a policeman's ball. The place was jam packed, it seemed like every cop in the city had come to pay their respects. I'm almost ashamed to say that I hardly knew anybody there, except the detective that had come by the house yesterday. He stood off to the side and just watched us as we accepted the condolences of Davis's friends and colleagues. It was amazing to see how many people's lives he touched. Even more amazing to see how many people he had fooled.

It still didn't seem real, it was like I was stuck in bad ass nightmare, but it was all too real. The comfort of all my stepdad's friends warmed my heart, and sickened me all at the same time. Then all of a sudden, I got that just much sicker! An ice-cold chill crept down my spine and I froze. Chance asked me what was wrong, he said "Baby you look sick, are you ok?" I thought I was about to swallow my tongue. It was Iesha, and right behind her was Tico. Everyone kept coming up hugging me and saying how sorry they were, but I couldn't hear a word they said. I was in a complete daze. You coulda' knocked me over with a feather! I began to sweat like I was wearing a full-length fur coat in 120 degree heat. Chance looked back over his shoulder. "Oh, hey Iesha, you made it. Good to see you." He said to Iesha as she walked over to me with Tico at her side, he was wearing a tacky ass orange suit. I almost threw up.

"Hey girl, hey Letah." Iesha said, hugging us both as Tico stood to the side grinning like Chester Cheetah.

"Hey Letah, hey Rayqelle, I'm sorry about y'all father. He was a great man. We will all miss him." Tico said as I started to tremble all over. "What's up man? How you doin'? I'm Tico Vega, a real good friend of the family. We all go way back. You must be Chance, I've heard alotta' about 'chu, yeah, a whole lot! ha-ha." Tico snickered as he reached out to shake Chances hand.

"Good to meet you Tico." Chance said, as he gave Tico the brother shake.

I was about to faint. What the fuck was this nigga' doin' here and what the fuck was he doing with Iesha?

Tico forced a fake casual conversation with Letah, her facial expression told me that she was just about to go off. I mean this nigga gon' prance up in here like ain't shit happen two days ago, like he ain't just tell me that he was fuckin' my seventeen year old baby sister, like she ain't HIV positive (probably 'cuz of his ass), and like he was just some old friend of the family. I wanted to hark somethin' up from the back of my throat and spit it right in his face! But I had to be cool and he knew it. If I had flipped out, Chance was gonna find out the whole truth today, for sure. Tico would make certain of that. I couldn't wait to talk to Iesha alone! She had alotta' nerve bringin' that piece of trash nigga' in here! What the fuck was she up to now?

CHAPTER 18

As the funeral service came to close, everybody started heading back to their cars, making their way to the cemetery for the burial. Me, Chance and Letah walked back to the limo. As we were about to get in, a big black Escalade with tinted windows pulled up next to us and came to a stop. The driver's side window rolled down. It was Tico "We just gon' follow behind y'all, wouldn't get lost, it's a long ways away, and we new in town. Ha-ha-ha!" He said through his big gold fronts. Iesha sat in the passenger's seat staring at me over the rim of her dark Chanel shades. The three of us got in to the limo and left for the graveyard. By the time we got there I was a complete nervous wreck trying to figure out what Tico and Iesha could possibly have up their sleeves. My hands were shaking like two autumn leaves. Chance touched me and held my hand, I instantly stopped shaking and for a moment everything was okay.

Letah and I walked over to the grave. It had been raining all morning, so our heels wedged themselves down inside the soft grass. We stood next to the casket as raindrops formed tiny pools on its surface and the preacher led us in prayer. "From ashes to ashes, from dust to dust." He said as Letah and I held hands, but we did not weep! Neither one of us could shed another tear.

Tico walked over and stood next to Chance, I was sickened and my stomach was doing flip-flops. I felt like I was about to shit on myself. Tico touched Chance's shoulder and whispered something into his ear. Chance looked over at me. I was frozen again! "What the fuck did he just say to him?" I thought. Iesha stood next to Tico, looking, hiding behind her shades. "Take those goddamn glasses off and look at me!" I thought, hoping without hope that she could read my mind. Everything went completely silent as the crank lowered Davis into the ground. Everything went black as if it were me being dropped into that burial vault. My heart broke all over again as I looked Letah, she and I held on to each other like two lost children. Chance walked up and stood behind me with his hand on my shoulder, he was my strength and just knowing that he was near made the pain a little easier to swallow.

We shook as many hands as we could before we got back into the limo to go home. Chance put his arm around me. I was so exhausted that I couldn't even speak. The only thing I can remember after that is waking up back at the house, stretched out on the couch, Chance was sitting on the floor next me. I guess he must have carried me in from the car, 'cuz I sure as hell couldn't remember walking! Letah was curled up in Davis's old lazy-boy, underneath an old cashmere blanket. Chance brought me over a sandwich and warm cup of tea, but I was too sick to eat. I was flooded with too many mixed emotions. Chance sat next to me all night and held my hand until the next morning.

I spent most of the next four or five days doped up on tranquilizers and the only time I got up was to pee. I couldn't eat, 'cuz I couldn't keep anything down. I just wanted to sleep, sleep the pain away. That was the only peace I could seem to get. I don't remember much about those few days, other than Chance being by my side everytime I woke up. I was a mess, I hadn't showered in days, finally Chance did insist on giving me a bath and thank God, 'cuz I must have smelled like the rear end of an ox.

By the sixth day, it was time for Chance to head back to Chicago and get ready for his art show, but I was in no condition to travel, so he made me stay on in San Diego, plus Linn had just gotten home from the hospital and needed my help. So, I drove Chance to the airport. He didn't wanna leave, I could see the worry all over his face, but I managed to pull it together enough to convince him that I'd be alright without him, for a few more days anyway. We kissed goodbye and Chance ran to make his flight. I wanted to cry as his plane took off, but I didn't have any tears left.

When I got back from the airport, I pulled in next to an expensive Jag that somebody had parked in the driveway and Letah's car was gone. When I got out and I walked into the house I almost lost my mind! There was Iesha sitting on the sofa in the living room. My purse fell to the floor.

"You bitch! What the fuck are you doin' in my house? And where the fuck is that nigga Tico? How the hell could you bring that mutha'fucka' to Davis's funeral?" I asked in outrage, surprised as hell that she would even have the nerve to show her face. Letah was gone out to run some errands and Linn was in the down stairs bedroom with her nurse.

"Hey Rayqelle, girl, I hope you don't mind, the nurse let me in, how you been? I've been calling you all week long! Didn't Chance tell you?" Iesha asked anxiously and as if nothing had ever happened.

"I've been sleepin' almost 24/7. Still tryin' to pull myself together, I guess. Still tryin' to cope, you know? My stepfather's death, missing my man, and girl stabbing me in the back!" I said, walking over to the mantle-piece, looking at an old family photograph.

"Look, I might as well get to the point. I know that you've been through a lot this week, but I need a huge favor." Iesha said as she walked up on me and stared into my eyes with an intense look.

"What?" I asked still in disbelief at this bitch's audacity.

"I have an important meeting scheduled for tomorrow in L.A. but I have to go back Chicago right away on an emergency." She said.

"Okay. So, what does that have to do with me? I asked, almost ready to punch her ass!

"Well, I need you to go to L.A. in my place and meet a client, it's very important and you are the only person I can trust to handle something like this. Like I said, I know you've been through a lot this week, but I really need your help." Iesha said as she turned slightly away to avoid looking me straight in the eye.

"Wait, what do you mean? What kinda' meetin'? And why me?" I asked as I began to get nervous.

"Well, it's more like a date, but it's super important or else I wouldn't be bothering you. I swear!" Iesha said.

" A date?" I asked. "What kinda date?" I asked as I already began to answer my own questions in my head. I already knew what kind of date. Suddenly I began to get nervous.

"My stepfather just died less than a week ago and you come here to ask me to go meet with one a' yo' tricks? What the fuck? " I said, as I grew more outraged!

"I know, and you know that I wouldn't even have come here if I didn't need you! Please, it'll only be this once! Come on girl, what do you say?" Iesha asked with all the nerve of a ghetto pit-bull.

"Let me get this straight, I'm less than one year away from earning my masters degree, I'm in love with the man of my dreams. For the first time in my life things are really lookin' up for me and you are askin' me to do what? Why the fuck would I wanna do some dumb shit like that?" I said, I could not believe what the fuck I was hearing!

"Let me make myself clear about something. I'm trying to be nice, but I'm not askin' you, I'm tellin' you!" Iesha said.

"I thought you were my supposed to be my girl! You ain't my friend, you couldn't be, tryin' to make me do some shit like this! You gotta' be outta' yo' mind. Get out! Just get the fuck outta' my sister's house!" I said growing more upset, I was about six seconds from stickin' my foot in her ass.

"Look. I'm runnin' outta' patience. This is a client that I can't afford to lose and I told you, it will only be this once. Rayqelle you know I wouldn't ask if I didn't really need you. I'm not tryin' to fuck up yo' game wit' that nigga! Please, I'm all for a bitch comin' up. I respect the game, shit, I was the one who schooled yo' lil prissy ass! Remember?" Iesha shouted.

"What game? First of all, I ain't runnin' no goddamn game! Those days are over! What I got wit' Chance is real and for the first time, I ain't gamin' nobody and ain't nobody gamin' me. I ain't about to fuck that up!" I shouted back.

"Do you even realize what would happen if Chance found out? I'm not doin' that shit! That might work out just fine for you, but that ain't even how I roll no more." I added.

"Rayqelle, Rayqelle, never kiss, never tell." She smiled and paused. So, what 'chu sayin' Bitch? You better than me now? You musta' forgot who you was, but I ain't forgot! You better remember where you came from! I seem to recall a time when yo' ass woulda' been more than happy to lay on yo' back fa' twenty or thirty minutes to get broke off a quick stack! But, now you gotcho' self a rich nigga and suddenly you Miss Goody Goody! You ain't nothin' but a ho', a expensive piece of pussy and I'm finna' prove it to you!" Iesha said as she quickly stomped over to the table in the corner of the living room and grabbed her Prada purse. She hastily opened it, reached in and pulled out a business card and walked back over toward me. My heart started to pound out of control!

"Be at the Airport Sheraton Hotel by L.A.X. tomorrow! You remember where that is don't you? You should, you turned enough tricks there." she asked sarcastically.

"That's all the way in L.A." I said.

"That's right, very good. You do remember. Make sure yo' ass is there by four o'clock and don't be late! Or I promise you, it's gon' be some drama! I would hate to have to call Chance lookin' for you and end up sayin' some shit that'll break his heart. Feel me? Oh, and fix yo' self up and do something wit'cho' hair. I can't have you makin' me look bad." Said Iesha smugly as she threw the business card in my face, "Oh and here's little something for your nerves in case you get jittery." She said as she tossed me a small vile of white powder and turned walking away toward the door, cracking it open just a bit. The card belonged to a Dr. Sadaaf Deepak, a neurologist from L.A.

"Who the fuck is this?" I asked.

"It's the client I was tellin' you about. Don't fuck this up, I'm dependin' on you!" Iesha said as she turned her head slightly, looking at me from the corner of her eye.

"Sadaaf Deepak? What, is he an Arab or somethin'?" I asked as if it really made any difference.

"No, Indian." She responded coldly as she walked out of the door, leaving it standing wide open behind her. I immediately dropped to my knees and began to cry. I cried so hard that I started to gag and vomit. And since I hadn't eaten in days, the only that came up was bitter acid from the very pit of my stomach. I was shakin' like a leaf, scared to death of what this bitch was about to drag me into.

I thought to myself. "Why would she want to pull me back into this shit? All we ever talked about was how one day we would get as far away from that life as possible.

Iesha knew where I came from and why I even started hustlin'. She knew it really didn't have a whole lot to do with the money, not necessarily. It was really a sickness, a twisted desire inside me to control somebody who thought they were controlling me. You see, what we used to do was find a guy with a lot of money, usually a hustla' that thought he was the shit and had money to burn or sometimes a doctor or a lawyer. Usually it was just about sex, other times they would really want a date, but the night almost always ended with sex, it was already set to go down that way.

Tico would hook it up. He had a team of ho's workin' for him, at first I was just one of 'em. I didn't actually become his woman until later. And even though I was his woman, I still had to pull my weight, just like the other ho's and I was so in love with the nigga that I woulda' did anything he told me to. And he use to always say "Pussy ain't shit! These mutha'fucka's can have yo' pussy, 'cuz I got'cho heart!" What he really meant to say was that he had my mind, and he knew that once he got control of a bitch's mind, the gamin' was easy.

The game was to meet mutha'fucka's wit money, get inside their of heads and then get inside of their wallets. My job was to meet 'em, impress 'em, then feed 'em some bullshit story about how hard it is out here and how I would not even be doin' this if I had a man to take care of me. Then that's when they usually turned into "Captain Save a Ho" and start talkin' 'bout how they can rescue you from yo' misery.

The shit makes me sick on the stomach to think about it!

I tried to think of anything I could to get out of this fucked up predicament that Iesha had put me in, but I also knew Iesha's potential for treachery, so I knew she wasn't bluffing about what she would say to Chance.

CHAPTER 19

The next day I arrived in L.A. at the Airport Sheraton hotel. I walked up to the front desk, told them my name and asked for room 2021. The clerk gave me a key card and pointed the way to the elevator. As I got in and closed the door I felt the butterflies in my stomach going crazy, I was about to come face to face with my worst nightmare! I was about to become a whore again! Everything I worked for, all I had been through, was all for nothing. In just a few short minutes I would be at the point of no return. My hands shook nervous as I dug through my purse looking for my compact to powder the sweat from my nose. Then, I saw the small vile of white powder that Iesha gave me incase I got jittery and I had never been more nervous! I had never fucked wit' cocaine before, it was the one thing I said I would never do, but then again, I also said that I would never turn another trick. Yet, there I was. So, I opened the small glass bottle, tipped it, dumping a little onto my pinky nail, and I snorted it, just as the elevator doors spread apart.

I arrived on the 20th floor and I stepped out, making my way down the long quiet hallway. I walked slowly and painfully, like I was on a Nazi death march. When I got to room 2021, I stopped, took a deep breath and knocked lightly on the beautiful cherrywood door. I had hoped to knock softly enough that who ever was on the other side might not hear even me and then I could just leave, but the door opened almost instantly. A woman answered.

"I'm sorry, I must have the wrong room. I was looking for Dr. Sadaaf Deepak." I said nervously, thinking that I had disturbed the wrong person.

"I am Dr. Deepak." The woman said as she smiled with the most gorgeous set of blinding-white teeth I had ever seen before in my life!

"But, you're a…" I said stumbling over my words.

"A woman?" She said as she smiled again, sensing my embarrassment.

"Did you not know that you would be meeting a woman today?" She asked kindly with the most beautiful accent.

"Well, uh… no, but I guess you did." I said.

"I hope this does not change anything, I was and still am greatly looking forward to…well, you know." She said as we both blushed uncomfortably.

"Please, come in." She said.

She was breath taking! She looked like an Indian goddess. She wore a beautiful red silk robe, the kind worn by the Japanese geisha girls. Her perfume was soft and sweet, and unfamiliar. Her skin was a flawless dark caramel, almost darker the mine and she wore hair up in a simple twist held together by a beautiful, long, golden hairpin. She couldn't have been more than twenty-nine or thirty years old, but she was a stunner! My heart pounded inside my chest like the kick from a bass drum as she held the door from me to come.

"You must be Rayqelle. You are even pretty than Iesha described!" She said as I entered the luxury suite. Her voice was as smooth as silk and her accent was like a cross between the queen of England's and a south-east Asian princess. I had been around all different kinds of people, rich, poor, intellectual, uneducated and I hardly ever let anybody intimidate me, but I knew class when I saw it and for the first time in along time, I felt out classed.

"Make yourself comfortable." She said. "You can change in the bedroom. I'll be out here. I have a few phone calls to make. So take your time."

So I went into the room and changed. I don't know if it was her soothing presence or the coke, but was starting to feel more and mellow.

When I came back out, all the lights had been turned down and in each corner, four softly scented tea candles burned. Sadaaf stood silently by the sofa.

"Come here." She whispered.

My stomach quivered nervously as the butterflies started up all over again.

I wore a white satin negligée with nothing underneath. She reached out her hand as I walked over to her. She slowly untied my robe and gently put her soft hands around my waist. Sadaaf moved closer and pressed her lips against mine, slowly working her way down to my breast. She massaged my while softly sucking and pulling at my nipples. Her tender touch quickly made my pussy wet and my clit started to swell and thump as I felt her reach between my legs.

We kissed again before she led me into the bedroom, holding one candle in her hand to light our way. She set the candle on the stand next to the bed.

"Please lay down on the bed." She said softly, getting behind me and guiding me by the small of my back onto the huge king sized canopy bed. She had taken full control of me, slowly turning my nervousness into burning desire. I leaned back on the soft egyptian-cotton sheets as she slowly spread my legs apart, running her fingers along my inner-thighs, following closely behind with soft kisses, until she reached my wetness. Her touch made me feel so good, her desire for me was over flowing!

She took her first two fingers and spread my pussy lips apart as she lightly flicked her tongue against my clit. Sadaaf took her time with me and loved me slowly, but my climax was coming fast. I reached down and ran my hands through her silky, black hair as she steadily sucked and kissed my swollen clit until I exploded. I pulled her up toward me, squeezing her full, beautiful breast. They looked like two ripe peaches that had been half way dipped in chocolate and my mouth watered as I gently sank my teeth in to her.

Sadaaf let her robe fall from her shoulders and on to the bed. I ran my fingers from her belly button down to her hairy treasure. She had taken her time to thoroughly pleasure me, so I felt it was only fair that I spend the rest of the evening doing the same in return. Especially since this evening was costing her two thousand dollars.

CHAPTER 20

Though Iesha promised that this would be the one and only time I had to this, she actually came to me several more times over the next few weeks with the same pressure ploy. Iesha was like a freight train that was speeding out of control. I could see her coming from a mile away, but I was tied helpless to the railroad tracks, unable to do a damn thing about it.

I had not talked to Chance more than once or twice in that two weeks and I knew that he was growing more and more suspicious. I had become an emotional and physical wreck. I had been taking tranquilizers during the day to help me sleep and cocaine to balance me out at night, so that I would be numb enough, but still up enough to do what ever she wanted me to do. Letah was the only person who knew what was going on and it was tearing her apart, because I now had her lying and covering up for me when I was out with a trick or when I was too sleepy or coked-out to deal with anybody, like Chance or Linn. She would just say that I was still having a tough time getting over Davis's death and that I was resting.

Another reason that I probably chose to hide behind the drugs was finding out that Davis had secretly been molesting Letah and that he was probably the person who had given her H.I.V. and not Tico like she had said earlier, in fact she may even actually infected him by accident when she ran away from home after I went away to grad school. So luckily I was never even exposed to the virus.

I never even had a clue, all the time believing that Davis was the last good man on earth. I felt so guilty that I had left her behind to suffer like that, Letah told me that the abuse started right around the time I started staying at grandma's. Letah said that she never told Linn what was going on either, because he had her so full of fear that if she did tell anybody, the courts would come along, split us all up and take us away and we would never see each other again. And Linn still didn't know, and there was no way to gage how she was going to react, after all that was her daddy, so we had both decided that it would be best to wait, Linn was still way too weak for any kind of drama and we didn't need anything sending her into a relapse.

It was all too much to deal with, things couldn't have gotten any worse, at least that's what I thought. By this time I had started to spiral downward and shit seemed more and more out of control. I hadn't seen Chance in weeks! I could barely even talk to him because I was so guilty about letting Iesha trap me into trickin' again. I couldn't eat, I had lost almost fifteen pounds, I had dark circles underneath my eyes and I was snorting so much coke that I was starting to bleed from my nose, but I couldn't stop 'cuz if I wasn't high on something my hands shook constantly! My mind and body were both falling apart and my soul was aching! I had done a lot of stupid shit when I was younger, I don't deny that, but the one thing I never did was fuck around with hard drugs. I drank and smoked weed here and there, depending on who I was around. Maybe Iesha and I might pop some "X" at a party, but I swore never to do anything hard like coke or heroin, because I saw the effect that it could have on people. I knew better or so I thought. Yet here I was, in two weeks I had become a stone-cold junky, a coke-head! I was on the verge of losing everything. Every trick had promised to be the last, but Iesha always had just one more trick for me to turn, just one more thing to do, she was never gonna stop! I had spent all those years perfecting the art of the hustle, only to end up as the one being hustled. Iesha had orchestrated a brilliant plan, she was using what I used to be to destroy all that I had become. I was caught between the proverbial rock and the ultimate hard place. Everything I had accomplished was at stake, and I could only see one way out. Iesha had to be dealt with! And she needed to be dealt with before I fell completely apart and before she got bored with this little game of cat and mouse and decided to tell Chance about my past, the past that she had again made my present.

I missed Chance like crazy, but I avoided talking to him as much as possible and I was growing more distant as each day passed. It was evident that something was wrong and he was getting more and more concerned and suspicious since I was normally too fucked up or depressed to hold any kind of meaningful conversation with him at all. Not to mention the fact that Letah was quickly running out of excuses. This was a man that I had spent everyday of the last three years of my life with and wouldn't have been apart from him for anything in the world. Now I was dodging him like I owed him money. I missed his touch, and the sexual encounters I was having brought me no personal satisfaction or pleasure, 'cuz ain't no love in trickin'! No matter how attractive they were, how nice or how rich, in the end it was just business and I was just a whore and Iesha had made herself my pimp. The very thing I was fighting to hold to was slipping right through my fingers! My Chance was slipping away!

Another week or so had passed and I was still avoiding Chance like the plague. I had only spoken to him once, and I was so high on tranquilizers that I could barely hold the phone. Letah was still covering my ass with excuse on top of excuse and she and I both knew that time was running out. She said that the last time she had spoken to Chance he sounded really anxious and she could tell that he was getting really fed up with excuses about why I was never able to come to phone and when I did, we didn't talk for more than a minute or so. She said that she hated lying to Chance because she really liked him and she knew everything I had been through and that I had finally found something real with him, something real that I was about ruin with all my lies.

CHAPTER 21

It was Friday night around eight o'clock, I had just woke up and was still trying to pull myself together. Iesha was throwing a party with some niggas from the Lakers, a couple of rookies with way too much money to burn. I was super groggy from all the pills I had taken early that morning to get to sleep. So, I stumbled over to the dresser 'cuz needed a baggy of dope to get me started. My hands were shaking outta' control, I needed a hit so bad. "If I could just keep my hands steady enough to line it up on the damn mirror!" I thought to myself as the doorbell rung and I about jumped outta' my goddamn skin, I was so jittery that I must have jerked and knocked the mirror on the floor with my coke on it. All the shit fell into the shag carpet, "aww, shit!" I shouted. As my stomach started to cramp. I went into an immediate panic, 'cuz that was the last bag and Iesha said she wouldn't be able to get any more until tomorrow, but I had to get through tonight. So I got down on my knees and drug my nose back and forth against the nap of the rug, trying to snort up what I could, when Letah frantically busted in the door, screaming like a maniac! "Bitch, what the fuck are you doin'? Get up off the floor! Chance is here, he is down stairs, right now! You better get yo' shit together and get it together quick! 'cuz he's ..." she shouted quietly before coming to a complete and awkward pause as she looked back, stunned, with her jaw dropped wide opened. Chance had been standing behind us in the doorway the whole time. I guess he was so excited to see me that he didn't wanna wait, so he decided to follow Letah up the stairs. She must have been so shaken up that she didn't even notice Chance following right behind her.

Chance was completely silent, as he looked at me. I was still bent over on my knees, my face close to the carpet with coke dust and dirt from floor stuck to my nose and upper lip. I was stunned like a deer caught in the headlights, and the look on my baby's face expressed the true nature of his confusion.

"Rayqelle, What's goin' on? What are you doin' on the floor?" Chance said as he stood perfectly still, trying to make sense of everything. I scrambled to my feet "Hey baby, why didn't you call and let me know you were comin'? Gimme a hug." I put my arms around him and held him tightly, but he just stood there. Then, he pulled away slightly, almost in horror. Chance stepped back and went into his jacket pocket, pulling out a napkin, reaching toward my face as I was started to bleed from one nostril. I snatched the napkin and turned away quickly to dab the blood from my nose. My hands were trembling and I was getting sick to stomach. I was standing in front of the man that I loved, the man I hadn't seen or really even talked to in weeks. And the only thing I could think about was the dope I had spilled in the carpet. My skin was starting to crawl, I needed a hit, bad! I was a broken mess! Letah politely excused herself and ran back down the stairs to check on Linn, she didn't wanna be any where insight when my shit hit the fan! Chance sat down in the chair by the cedar chest. "Why haven't you been returning my calls? What's goin' on with you?" he asked.

"I've just been goin' through alot since my stepfather died, just so many things goin' on inside my head. But I'm o.k. I'll be fine." I said, still agonizing over the last bag of coke I had so clumsily spilled a few minutes before. I was trippin'! I wanted to get back down on my knees and lick that spot on the rug that held the last bit of dust.

"Why are you sweatin' like that? Are you sick? And what were you doin' on the floor like that? And why does your nose keep bleeding?" Chance asked as he reached for me again, I snatched away. I didn't want him too close to me, I felt dirty and ashamed. I felt like he could see right through me.

"Sit down and talk to me, I have not seen you in over a month! Why do you keep squirmin' and dancin' around? Seriously, are you alright?" he asked again, getting more impatient.

"I'm fine!" I snapped. " I ... I ... I just need some water! Will you go downstairs and get me some? And get it from the faucet, and let it run for a few minutes, so it gets nice and cold." I said, trying to think of anything to get him out of the room for a minute.

"The faucet?" he asked. "You don't even drink faucet water." He added, looking even more confused.

"Please! Chance, just go ... and get... the water!" I said, almost begging. Chance looked at me with greater confusion, turning slowly and walking out of the door. I shut it behind him and quickly dashed over to the phone by the bed to call Iesha, she had to know somebody who could get their hands on some more coke. I dialed her number and the phone rang.

"Whaz-up, girl? You ready for this party? She asked. "Better brace yo' self, I hear he's got a dick the size of a California cucumber." She added.

"Iesha, listen, I'm gon' need some more coke, I spilled the last baggie on the floor, when Chance rang the doorbell, and..." I tried to explain as she cut me off.

"Chance, what the fuck is he doin' here? You better tell that nigga, you got plans tonight!" Iesha said.

"Plans? I can't just tell him that I have plans, he came all the way from Chicago and he's my fiancé." I said as my stomach churned and my body ached!

"Not for long, not if you fuck this up! These niggas are paying me good money for that ass! Chance can have what's left of it after they get finished!" Iesha barked into the phone like the bitch she was.

"What about the coke, I need some bad! Right now. Please I'm gettin' sick!" I begged Iesha.

"Bitch, coke? What coke? You mean that white powdered courage you been snortin' up like you was crazy? You stupid ho, that was china white, not coke! That was heroin!" Iesha said as she laughed uncontrollably.

"Heroin? Why the fuck would you gimme some shit like that? You scandalous bitch! You got me hooked on heroin? You said that was cocaine! You said it was just coke!" I screamed into the phone in pure terror!

"No, bitch! You said it was coke! You got yo' self hooked, not me. You are one that was suckin' up that shit like vacuum cleaner! I even told yo' ass to slow down. But I know one thing, you had better be ready by eleven o'clock or I'm gon' fuck you up, fa'real and after I get finished, I'm gon' sit yo' rich nigga down and tell him a little story. All about yo' nasty ass. So get it together! Brent Williams is gonna be waitin'!" Iesha shouted into the phone. "That's why I don't fuck wit' dope fiends!" Iesha said to someone in the back ground as slammed the phone in my ear.

I started to cry. The shakes were getting worse, much worse! I was sweatin' like a run away slave and my stomach was crampin' like a mutha'fucka'. I was so sick that I never even realized that Chance had come back up the stairs and was standing in the doorway behind me with tears in his eyes. I stood up slowly and walked toward him. He stood motionless but he exuded more emotion than I was able to stand. He had heard the entire conversation, so there was really no need to try and make up anymore lies. It had been a crazy ass six weeks, and what was really crazy is that I did all this shit to hold on to the one thing that had come to mean the world to me, only to still end up about to lose it anyway. My world was crumbling right before very eyes!

"Who was that on the phone?" he asked.

"It was Iesha, she was ..." I tried to answer.

"She was what? Stuffin' yo' nose wit' dope? What the fuck is wrong with you? You look terrible! And Iesha did this to you? Why? Just tell me why. Wasn't she supposed to be yo' girl?" He asked, as he stared at me with a sobering mix of utter confusion and complete disappointment, struggling to understand.

"So is this what you been doin' wit'cho' self the last six weeks, hangin' out wit'cho' yo girl gettin' high? Is this why you can never take my calls, why you been avoiding me like the plague? I had started to think you met somebody new, but I guess it wasn't a somebody, just something." His strong voice shuttered with intense hurt, and the sad part is that he didn't even know the half of it. Not only was

I now a junky, I was also a liar and whore, he just didn't know it yet. If he thought he felt like crying now, wait until he had heard it all! 'Cuz in about two hours I was gonna have to leave here, that's when really it's gon' go down. But before I could deal with anything, I was gonna have to get a fix and quickly! Apparently I was goin' through some sort of withdrawal from some shit I didn't even know I was using. Since I had never used cocaine or heroin before, I had no idea what either one of them was supposed to feel like, all I knew was that it felt good and made the shit Iesha had me doing go down a whole lot easier. Tonight was the first time I had to be without it since I started using and I was not doing well at all.

Chance sat down on the bed and shook his head in disbelief, covering his face with both hands. He laid his head back on the oversized pillows. Devastated by what he had just learned and exhausted from jet lag, Chance closed his eyes, took a deep breath as he relaxed his head on the pillow. I watched him breathe as he laid perfectly still, , his strong chest rose and fell as he began to drift off to sleep. And before I know it he was snoring. I sat on the floor next the bed, wanting to touch him, but I knew that this my chance to slip out and do what I had to do. So I made sure not to wake him, then I grabbed my purse and some clothes. I knew that if I timed this right I could be out and back before Chance even realized that I was gone. I quietly crawled out of the door, gently closing it behind me. Then I carefully tip-toed down the stairs and ran over to wake Letah. Who was sleeping on the couch. I touched her softly on the shoulder so as not to startle her. I quickly explained to her that Iesha had been giving me heroin instead of cocaine and that was why I was getting sick and had to go find some more right away or I was gonna die, at least that's what it felt like anyway. Letah beg to go with me, but I told her that I needed her to stay here in case Chance woke up before I could get back, if he got up and found me gone, I needed Letah to be here to try and keep him calm, as much as she was able. Fortunately Chance was a hard sleeper, and when he was out, he was usually out for the count! So Letah agreed to stay behind, but I told her to call me right away if Chance woke up. And if she had to tell him anything, just to tell him that I just went for a drive and that I would be right back.

So I jumped in the car and put it in neutral, letting it roll out of the driveway slowly, down to the end of the street, I didn't want to draw any more attention to the fact that I was leaving. I started the engine as soon as got the second corner and quickly sped away. Linn lived in the Kensington District of San Diego, one of the nicer areas of the city, so I knew there was no place around there to buy any dope. I mean it wasn't like the hood, where there was a friendly neighborhood street pharmacist standing on every corner ready to serve. I had to get to City Heights, one of the roughest ghettos in southern California and it was no place to take lightly, especially at night! I did sixty the whole way there. I mean, I made it all the way from Kensington, to 43rd and Fairmont in twelve minutes, with out getting pulled over by the cops, that had to be one for the Guiness Book of world records. When I pulled up, there were three Latin Gangstas posted up against the side of a run down building. One of them saw that I was sitting there at the stop sign trying to get there attention, they figured that I either had to be a cop, or some boozhee bitch from El Cerrito or somewhere, trying to score some dope. Then, one of them said something to the other two in Spanish and they all laughed.

"Whaz-up ma? What 'chu need baby?" The little dark haired thug said as he walked over and leaned into the driver's side window of the car, looking around and then into the back seat to make sure I wasn't five-0.

"I need some china white!" I said nervously. I couldn't believe what I was doing!

"China White? Goddamn ma! You fuckin' wit dat real shit! You gotta be outta yo...!" He said as I abruptly cut him off.

"Mutha'fucka, do you got it or not?" I shouted at the dark haired gangsta! By then I was really starting to feel the effects of the withdrawals and my patience was running short, but for a minute I musta' forgot what type of person I was dealing with, because before I could finish my sentence the latin gangsta had pulled a gun from up under his white-T and wedge it in between my chin and neck. I was already sweating like I had just run the miracle mile, but now my sweat ran cold as I watched my life flash before me.

"Better pump yo' brakes bitch! I should rob yo' pretty ass, but know what I'm gon' do instead? I'm gon' hook you up wit' this real shit! Yeah, cuz once you get a hit a' this, you gon' be in love, everytime you get a dollar you gon' be runnin' back to El Cajun to holla' at me. So, see bitch, I ain't even gotta' rob you, 'cuz I'm already in yo' pockets and soon as yo' money run out, I'm gon' be up in that lil' tight pussy a' yours." He said, grinning and looking back at his homeboys.

So, I made the buy and sped the fuck outta' El Cajun. I was aching all over, my nose was running and I had the worst case of chills. I could barely see straight enough to drive. I only made it as far as 47th and Meade before I had to pull over and stop to take my medicine. I looked around, making sure nobody was walking by and that no cops were rolling through. Once I made sure the coast was clear I took the key out of the ignition and stuck it down into the plastic. I scooped out some powder, and put it upto my nose and snorted, once, then twice, and then again. I felt the dust hit my sinus and start to tingle, I sneezed, and then... almost immediately I felt the calm, the rush, as the aches started to subside, my pain got further and further away. I leaned forward in the seat, focusing on the Acura symbol in the center of the steering wheel. I started to nod, I could feel it all over, I was free!

Then my cell phone rang, almost scaring me to death! One ring, two rings, three rings, I heard it clearly, but I couldn't move. I was fucked up! The phone rang again, one ring, two rings, then another, then I shook myself and grabbed for the phone that was laying in the passengers seat.

"H.. he.. hell...Hello." I struggled to speak.

"Bitch, where you at?" It was Iesha.

"I ... I ... had to go get some .." I was too fucked up for words, I just wanted to enjoy my high while it lasted.

"Bitch, I told you, I had something for you to do tonight! It's eleven-thirty, do you want me to fuck you up? 'Cuz I will. Look, these niggas are waitin' on you, get 'cho ass downtown, now! You got thirty minutes!" Iesha hung up the phone. By then she had blew my high wit' all that yellin' and shit. But at least I was starting to feel well again. So I decided to go ahead to the hotel, I figured I would run in, smile, walk around and look pretty and give one or two mutha'fuckas some head, maybe fuck 'em real quick, if I just had to and then be on my way. I could be back to the house with Chance before he even missed me.

CHAPTER 22

When I got to the hotel, I made my way up to the penthouse and rang the bell. The door opened and there stood Iesha, wearing a short pink nighty and matching high heels. There were three other girls in sexy lingerie, sandwiched between three tall, fine ass, muscle bound niggas (all rookie NBA players) sitting on an oversized white sofa in the living room. Each guy had his own bottle of Crystal in his hand, waving it around as they argued and debated back and forth, screaming over music that was too loud, about who had gotten the biggest signing bonus and trying to out floss each other in front of their paid companions. I went on in to the back and undressed, quickly getting in the shower to wash the funk from my body where I had sweated in agony, crying out for the bitter china white. The hot water beat down on my neck and back, almost soothing the soreness of my soul.

I got out and got dressed, slipping into a little sexy number that I had bought along time ago for Chance but never got to wear.

I stopped and looked in to the full length mirror that was very carefully placed to capture a view of the king sized bed, checking my hair and make up, adjusting my cleavage before making my entrance. Then Iesha stormed in!

"Hurry up! I need yo' ass out there, not in here!" She said as she stood with both hands placed upon her curvaceous hips. I took one last look in the mirror, hating what I saw, but vowing that this would be the last night for anymore of this kind of shit.

CHAPTER 23

I opened the door and walked out into the living room. Each one of the girls turned and looked at me as if I was public enemy number one, guarding the nigga they sat with, as if I come to steal their thunder. Little did either one of them know, I couldn't have been less interested in either one of those niggas. I was just trying to get through this night the best way I could, hopefully without having to be kissed, fuck or fondled in the process. Ironically not one of those niggas paid me one bit of attention. So, I spent the next four hours listening to four self indulged, over sized niggas tell a bunch of over exaggerated basketball stories and over the top tales about what they bought, what they had done and what they were about to do, it was all I could do to keep my fuckin' eyes open! Two of the niggas ended up passed out on the couch drunk, one went off to a private suite with two of the girls and the other one disappeared into another one of the back rooms with Iesha. I was just sorta' sitting there by myself, watching

MTV Cribs. So, quietly I grabbed my shit and proceeded to bounce the fuck up out'a there.

I walked exhaustedly down the long hallway of the twenty fifth floor on my way to the elevator and on my way to what felt like new found freedom, that I was grasping for at all cost. As I stood impatiently waiting for the elevator to reach my floor, I heard a clicking sound coming from the door situated to the right of me, it was the sound of the latches opening and the doorknob turning. I could also hear someone exchanging words, it sounded like two men arguing in a hushed tone. What ever was going on I didn't wanna know about it. So, I put my head down so that I wouldn't have to make any eye contact with whoever was about to open that door, I was still half wasted and starting to come down off the heroin that I snorted earlier and really didn't feel like faking any smiles or small talk as they passed me. Then the door opened, I could see from my peripheral vision that it was dark inside, and a large white man walked out. From a quick glance I saw that he was carrying what looked like an ice bucket. I thought it was a bit peculiar that he had left the door standing wide opening, but white people do weird some shit and I had enough problems of my own to worry about, and "maybe he left it open on purpose." I thought as he passed behind, my back still turned to avoid all eye contact. Then, as I reached out again to press the down button, I noticed that the man's footsteps had stopped almost right behind me and then before I could turn around, I felt a great jolt against my back and then I heard a crackling sound, like electricity. I had been shocked with some kind of taser! Then a strong hairy arm clamped itself down around my neck, almost crushing my windpipe and choking the life out of me as he dragged me backward into the room that sat next to the elevator. Once inside, someone standing behind the door quickly slammed it shut and the room went pitch black. "Ain't this a bitch!"? I thought, hearing the ding from the elevator open as it had finally arrived, ten seconds too late!

I felt myself losing consciousness; I hadn't had any air in over thirty seconds. It may not sound like a long time, but try doing it while your kicking and fighting for your life. I managed to get in one quick, precious breath as the man repositioned his grip around my neck. I couldn't see, but I heard the footsteps as they got closer and then something hit me in the face, it felt like a hammer with skin around it, but I guess it was the fist of the other man in the room. I could tell it was a man, because I heard him grunt as kick and beat me, over and over and over again, while the man from the hallway held me. "It's my turn." He said as he pushed me to the floor and stood on top of me until the other man could get his arms around me from behind and pick me up. Then, the beating started again. The second guy punched me in my stomach again and again, knocking the wind out of me until almost passed out. Then I heard what sounded like third person moving toward me from the opposite side of the room, his footsteps grew closer until he stood right in front of me, so close I smell his funky breath and the cologne he wore was strangely familiar. But I was so terrified that I just couldn't place it. I trembled as the room went dead silent and then he whispered into my ear "Told you I was gonna have this pussy!" as he reached between my legs and jammed his fingers inside me. It was over for me! I must have passed out.

When I woke up I was in the hospital, I could only see a little light peeking through a small crack that use to be my eye. I struggled to get to my feet, but two nurses held me down and tried to restrain me. My eyes were swollen shut from the severe beating I had just endured. Letah and Chance stood on both sides of the bed, holding my hands, saying, "It's alright calm down, you're safe now, everything is ok!" but I didn't know where my attackers were and since I had no idea who they were, I was still in a panic!

"Chance!" I called to him.

"Oh my God!" Chance gasped after seeing my bruised and swollen face when the nurse shined the bright light on to me. "I'm gon' kill that jealous bitch!" He said.

"Chance, I'm so sorry! Please let me explain!" I said.

"I already learned more than I ever wanted to know. But one thing is for sure, Iesha has gotta pay for everything she did, to you, and to us!" Chance shouted as he stormed out of the room. I called to him over and over, but he wouldn't answer. I could hear his footsteps grow more faint as he hurried away.

Chance stormed out of the hospital, jumped into his car and sped off. He was heated and had only one thing on his mind. That was finding Iesha. He looked at the crumpled note on the napkin and grew more and more angry. Beads of sweat dripped from his head. He didn't know what he was gonna do when he got there, he just knew that he wanted to make her pay for what she had done.

The wheels of the car came to a screeching halt inside the underground garage of the hotel. Chance looked at the crumpled piece of paper on his lap with Iesha's room number and phone extension. Chance grabbed his cell phone and angrily mashed Iesha's cell phone number into his phone, and then he waited as it rang over and over again. There was no answer, so he tried once more, and still no answer. Then he decided to dial her room directly since he had the extension number right in front of him. He dialed the hotel main number and then asked to be connected to ext. 1100. The phone rang but there was no answer. His frustration grew.

CHAPTER 24

Chance was sick of waiting! So he decided to get out of the car and make his way up to Iesha's suite. His heart pumped and he could feel the blood course through his veins. He looked around the ground floor of the parking garage to make sure that there was no one around. Then walked quickly and steadily toward the elevator, but he thought to himself that he should take the stairs to be on the safe side. He quietly opened the door to the stairwell, holding the handle so as not to let it slam shut behind him and carefully pounced up 11 flights of stairs, taking two to three steps at a time. Exhausted and gasping for air, he reached the floor, opened the door to the hallway and discreetly entered! He knew what he had in mind and that he didn't want any witnesses.

Chance moved swiftly down the long hall, with a blood focus on the double oak doors trimmed in gold that lay directly ahead. The closer he got the more his blood boiled! He had never been so angry, so disrespected or so violated. "Nobody is about to destroy my life and get away with it!" He said to himself. All his thoughts came to a head as he approached Iesha's suite and banged on the huge oak grain door. He knocked once and then again. "Iesha, open the mutha'fuckin' door! I'm about to teach yo' stank ass a serious lesson! You should'a never fucked wit' what was mine!" Chance shouted as he slammed his fist against the hard wood. Then he wrapped his hand around the doorknob and shook the door as hard as he could, and with one firm twist of the handle, the door inched open. Chance stood at the crack of the opening, peering in. "Iesha!" Chance called aloud. "Bitch, I know you hear me!" Chance pushed the door open, cautiously looking around the huge living room from outside the door.

He stepped inside, still calling out to Iesha, with no response. The big screen television blared loudly and music thumped from the behind the bedroom door. Something was wrong, something just didn't feel right, but he was mad as hell, so he stormed over to the door and shouted one more time. "Bitch, come out here! I'm about to fuck you up!" When there was no answer Chance turned the handle and flung open the door and rushed inside the dark room.

He slipped and fell, "Damn, what the fuck?" he said, "What's this shit all over the floor?" thinking maybe someone had spilled juice or champagne. He got up, even more pissed off now after falling and getting his clothes all wet. He walked back over to the doorway and felt along wall for a light switch, and flipped it on. Chance began shake as a cold chill ran down his spine, standing frozen in horror, he looked around the room and gasped.

It was like a seen out of Friday the 13th, there was blood every where, splattered all across the walls and ceiling, and where he thought he had slipped and fallen on some spilled juice or champagne, it was a puddle of blood with Iesha laid in the middle. She was cut wide open, from her neck down to her pelvis, all her insides exposed! She wore a white satin negligee that had been stained the color of crimson. Chance trembled! Everything was covered in blood, now even himself from where he had fallen into the middle of the macabre mess. Chance was immediately seized by panic, scrambling quickly out of the room but again falling into the slick pool of blood. He tracked through the living room, up to the foyer and out of the front door, stamping bloody footprints all along the shiny marble floor behind him. Back into the hallway, out of the door and down the stairwell. He made his way down the eleven flights in half the time it took to him get up.

Chance dashed down the last flight of stairs in the hotel with intense fear, the front of his clothes covered with blood, leaving crimson handprints smeared all along the wall and banister behind him. As he reached the bottom of the dimly lit stairwell, he quickly headed toward the back entrance and scrambled out of the huge, rusty steel door marked emergency exit. Chance could hardly catch his breath, so he stopped a moment and kneeled forward with sweat pouring from his face. He struggled to figure out what to do, where to go, who to call and how he got caught up in such a helluva' mess. As the sound of approaching sirens grew closer,

Chance dipped back to the car, jumped in and pulled out of the dark parking garage. In complete shock Chance sped down a dark back alley, disappearing completely into the night.

All that night doctors and came in and out checking on my condition, a police detective showed up asking a bunch a questions that I was ready or able to answer. I just could not get my mind off Chance, it had been over three hours and we still hadn't heard a word from him. I was worried sick. I spent a major part of that night answering questions from the police and there wasn't a while lot I could tell 'em, except that I was snatched into a room where I got beat the fuck up by two white guys. I was in pretty bad shape: I had a concussion, two broken ribs, a dislocated shoulder and a bruised kidney, but through it all there was only one thing on my mind, and that was Chance!

CHAPTER 25

While being questioned by the police, a special all points bulletin came over the radio. It was in regard to a murder at the Omni Hotel, "the victim was a 27 year old African American female, with California drivers license DJ01478L registered to an Iesha Ellis of Los Angeles." It went on to say that the victim had been badly mutilated and a suspect was wanted for questioning in connection with the murder, 25 years old Evan Chance of Chicago, Illinois. The suspect was described as an African American male, about 6'1" in height, 185 pounds, with dark brown skin, bald headed with no facial hair, and a slim to muscular. Approach with caution!"

The detective turned his eyes slowly toward me. "Miss Davis didn't you say that your boyfriends name was Chance, Evan Chance?" He asked.

My heart began to pound against my chest like a sledgehammer as sweat poured from my brow. "Yes! But he is not a murderer! He could never do anything like this! You need to be out there lookin' for the mutha'fuckas that did this to me, you find them and I bet you'll find Iesha's killer. Chance did not do this!" I exclaimed through my loose teeth and swollen upper lip.

"Where is he?" The detective asked calmly.

Letah and I both looked and each other, remaining quiet. The silence in the room was thick enough to cut with a knife! And then ...

"Don't play with me! This is not a fuckin' game! Your boyfriend is out there with a warrant for his arrest, and an approach with caution advisory over his head. That means if he even so much as sneezes, some nervous ass rookie cop is probably gonna blow his mutha'fuckin head off his shoulders! Is that what you want? Now, tell me where he is!" The detectives voice broke through the dead silence like a brick through a plate glass window! And I fell to into small piece.

"I don't know, I swear! But he'll be back here to see about me, he wont stay away with me here! Please don't hurt him!"

The detective grabbed his cell phone, punching the life out of the buttons! "This detective Rick Connor at Sharp Memorial working the Davis assault case. Hey listen, I just got a possible lead on the Iesha Ellis murder case..." I was sick to my stomach as he coldly and matter of factly spoke to who ever was on the other end. He talked about Chance like he was talking about an animal they were hunting!

Unknown to all of us, Chance had gone back to the house to get some clean clothes and, to talk to Linn, to try and explain everything that happened. Still in the car, he sat in the driveway and leaned back in the seat to catch his breath for a moment. The first thing that he wondered was, who could have done this to Iesha, second thing he thought was, how badly he had wanted to hurt her for what she had done to us, and that his intentions were to go over there and fuck her up. Somewhere deep down inside he was glad that he didn't, but he wasn't the least bit sorry for her. After all, if she had been any where near as foul to anybody else as she had been to me, she had it coming. He just hated that fact that he had to be the one to walk smack dab into the middle of the shit, literally!

Chance was so tired, physically, mentally and in every other way you could image from all the shit I had taken through over the past two months, so he put his head back against the seat and closed his eyes. Just then he heard a click as he opened his eyes to find the end of a nine-millimeter handgun pressed up against the side of his head. It was a deputy from the San Diego County Sheriff's Department. "Evan Chance, you are under arrest for suspicion of murder, put your hands on the steering wheel and don't move!

At the same time Linn was also placed under arrest for Davis's murder. They carefully placed her inside an ambulance and escorted her to the infirmary at the Justice Center, where she gave a full confession. It turns out that she had been slowly poisoning my stepfather with arsenic, because of all the medications he was on, it was difficult to distinguish the difference between possible drug interaction and him actually being poisoned until an autopsy was performed. The detective asked why she did it and here it what she said.

The day that Lady-Bird died, Linn was at home with her. They had been playing hide and go seek when Davis came home for lunch, that's when him and Lady-Bird started to argue, Linn said that she heard her tell Davis that she knew what he had been doing to Letah and she was gonna go to the police. Linn said that Davis told LadyBird that he would kill her first and then he put his hands around her neck, strangling her to death. Then he picked her up and took her into my room, placed a rope around her neck and hung her from the wood beam in the ceiling. Linn was behind the door hiding, he never even noticed her.

I'm laying in that hospital bed bruised and battered, then that fuckin' cop was getting' on my nerves askin' all those damn questions and going out of my mind with worry about Chance and on top of all this, now I was starting to go into withdrawals again. It had been close to 12 hours now since my last fix, so the cramps and fatigue were kicking back in. It felt like I was itching inside and I couldn't keep still! The only thing that was really saving me from going completely nuts was the morphine drip they had me on for the pain. But I still needed a hit, my body craved it! And in a short while I knew I would be crying for it! So, I begged Letah to go out to the car and get the stash that I had bought earlier last night. She didn't want to, but I insisted, so she finally gave in, only after I promised on LadyBird's grave that this would be the last time.

While I waited on her to get back, I figured I would turn on the TV to pass time. I clicked the remote control until I landed on channel 8. Then, I just about swallowed my tongue! There was a picture of Chance being broadcast in connection Iesha's murder. The reporter was saying something about investigators finding Chance's fingerprints at the scene and surveillance video from the hotel at the time of the murder showing him entering and leaving her suite. They also said that this was particularly gruesome crime and something about the murderer having removed Iesha's heart from her chest. They also said that chance was being held at the San Diego County Detention Center on a one million cash dollar bond. They were also saying some crazy shit about this being his second time he had been charged for murder. They said the first time that the case was thrown out due to a hung jury or something. He supposedly beat some guy to death in 2001, a football player from N.K.U at a college party. I was in a complete state of shock! What they were just saying could not have been true, Chance and I had been together for over three years and he never even so much as raised a hand to me and I'm supposed to believe that he killed somebody six years ago and never mentioned anything about it. Letah stood at the entrance to the door where she had standing for about the past five minutes. I didn't even notice, she walked over to me slowly as I began to cry. "If I had only told Chance the truth about my past when we met none of this would be happening. It's all my fault!" I said. "Looks like you both had some skeletons in the closet." Letah said as she reluctantly handed me the small baggy of heroin and nervously stood watch while I quickly snorted the "real" pain medicine. And like magic, the ache left me as I eased back into the bed and prepared to take flight for one last time. You see, I promise Letah that I was gonna tell my doctor that was hooked on dope, so that I could start some kind of treatment right away. I had too much to live to go out like this! And then ...

About twenty minutes later I went into heart failure and slip into comma due to a bad interaction from the mixture of heroin and morphine. The doctors worked on me for the next two hours, but it was no use. I died at 8:47pm. The toxicology report showed high amounts of heroin in my bloodstream, cause of death was rule an overdose, enough to kill a horse they said.

Even with all of his family's money and influence behind him, Chance spent the next two weeks in police custody, the district attorney managed to convince the judge that he was a flight risk and an extreme threat to the community, so his bond was revoked. Shortly after that some new evidence was introduced that proved Chance's innocence and cleared him on all charges, so he was finally released. With his life shattered and his heart broken into a thousand pieces over my death, he returned back to Chicago, placed his house up sale and disappeared, nobody has seen or heard from him since. My fear and my lies destroyed the only man I ever loved!

Apparently Frank Jordan the Congressman from Chicago that Iesha was gamin', finally got wise and when he figured out that he could never really have her, no matter how much he loved her or how much that he gave her, he had some of his goons track her down and wipe her out. He had fallen deeply in love with her and was determined to have her heart, one way or another, so he had his boys remove it from her body and bring it to him, he said, "that way, he knew he would always have it." One of the men that was paid to kill her suddenly found religion and developed a conscience, ain't that a bitch! He blew his own brains out, but before he did, he left a note confessing to God and to man every filthy deed he had ever committed. Among

them was Iesha's brutal murder. The Cook
County district attorney's office immediately
issued a search warrant for the
Congressman's home, there they found all
the evidence they needed to gain an
indictment on a capital murder charge, in
addition to a felony charge for gross abuse
of a corpse. They also arrested the other
fools who were responsible for Iesha's
death, among them was my ex-boyfriend
Tico, it turns out that he had actually met
the Congressman through Iesha when he
got out of prison, he was hired to handle
some of the Congressman's "dirty" street
business. Tico also admitted to attacking
me at the hotel that same night, he said
that it was payback for setting him up,
which I did in order to escape him 4 years
ago. It also turns out that Tico was actually
the one who cut Iesha open and removed
her heart (while she was still alive!) He told
her that this was payback for all the hearts
she had stolen in her life. I always knew
that he was a cold-blooded mutha'fucka,
but what he did to Iesha was just sick! I
guess the "chance she took" ended up
costing her dearly! Just like mine ultimately
cost me everything that I had cherished

and waited so long for, my peace, my happiness, my new life and my "Chance".

Come visit me at

www.myspace.com/1koleblack

HERE IS A PREVIEW OF THE NEXT
EXCITING NOVEL FROM *KOLE BLACK*!

At The Risk of Chance

At The Risk of Chance

The right chance could make you risk it all

CHAPTER 1

As the September rains began to fall, I stood outside on the patio staring at the ocean with tears in my eyes. I watched the waves crash against the sandy shoreline of the beach as the wind started to pick up. It was hurricane season in Miami.

From behind me, I heard the sound of the glass patio door slide open. It was Chance. I heard his footsteps move toward me, but I never turned around. I didn't want him to see that I had been crying again, but he didn't need to see my face, because he always knew when I was hurting. He could just feel it!

Chance walked up and stood right behind me. With my back still turned, he put his arms around me and held me close to himself, as he softly kissed my neck and shoulder. A heavenly chill went down my spine. He had never touched me this way before! His hands were warm and strong. His kisses were tender. I was comforted instantly. His touch sent a rush all the way through me. He made my whole body hot! I had been waiting for this for so long!

I turned around to face him. Then, with out even so much as a single word, he slowly pressed his soft, full lips against mine. I reached up and slid the tips of my fingers against his smooth baldhead, as the rain washed over us both. His arms tightened around me like two steel bands that I could not have escaped, even if I had wanted to. Which I didn't, not even in the least!

Slowly I ran my hands underneath his soaking wet tank top as the rain started to pour and he squeezed me even tighter. Our eyes locked, as the wind blew and the storm began around us! I reached out and touched his chest and proceeded to slide my hands all over his hard, muscular frame. His pecks rippled and flexed as he grabbed me around the waist and lifted me up on to the wooden patio guard railing, kissing and biting me on the neck, while I grew hotter and hotter!

Then he wrapped his fist around the collar of my t-shirt and ripped it straight down the middle, exposing both of my breasts. He held them in his hands and licked the droplets of rain from my nipples. I was under his complete control! I put my arms around his neck as he tore my panties apart at the seams and snatched them off of me. He put his arms back around me and kissed me deeply as I reached down into his shorts. I gasped as I touched his manhood. It was so long and so hard! "Hell, who am I kidding?" It was huge! We were both now ready.

Chance then braced himself firmly against me. Our bodies pressed against one another, my dark brown skin melted against his dark brown skin. I could feel it as my body screamed his name out loud. He was my fantasy! The fantasy that had played over and over again inside my head for the past year. He was everything to me! He was all that I had known, and this was going to be my ultimate expression of love. This was our first time!

My clitoris thumped out a peculiar beat as I took the tip of his dick between my fingers and wedged it against the juicy entrance of my vagina. I was throbbing! I wanted it, but I was scared! Chance sensed my fear and paused, looking deeply into my eyes through the constant downpour of rain. I kissed his lips and took the deepest breath of my life, as he pushed himself inside me.

I wrapped my legs around him as he picked me up off of the wood railing, slowly stroking me back and forth. I then put my arms around his neck as he held me up in the air and stroked me. I squeezed his massive arms as they flexed harder than two iron rods. With his hard dick still inside me, he carried me into the house, grunting as he forcefully slid the glass patio door back open as he made his way over to the white cushioned wicker sofa in the sunroom that faced outward at the beach, where the storm pounded the foamy surf against shore.

Chance laid me down on the sofa and stepped out of his boxers, with his dick sharply at attention. I could still smell the sweet sea breeze as it blew in through the open door. I could still hear the waves crashing outside almost in perfect time with the sound of my own beating heart, while Joe sang "If I Was Yo' Man" over the Bose Stereo System.

Chance kneeled down before me and kissed me and then moved down to my neck, my titties, my stomach and then he kissed my thighs as he parted my legs. Then he began to softly French kiss my pussy, slowly and deeply. I came almost right away! I started to moan out of control as he took his time and tasted every single drop of my love. Every little drip drop!

After what had to be two or three of the most intense orgasms known to man, Chance pulled himself up toward me at eye level and slowly worked his dick back inside me. It was so intense that I could not help but dig my nail inside his dark chocolate skin. And he dug himself deeper inside me. I shuttered as he tapped what I guess was my "G-Spot"! Over and over and over again!

Then, he put my legs up in the air and began to fuck me slowly, taking his time. Pushing his dick all the way inside me and then pulling it all the way out, again and again. I was in the sweetest of agony and the river that flowed from inside me was the proof. I would have never imagined that I could feel so good. My heart began to race out of control and my pussy started to quiver in an unusually intense spasm. I wanted to scream but I couldn't catch my breath!

Chance plunged and thrust himself inside me, until he started to go into his own ecstatic spasm and then he squeezed me and shouted out loud "Oh, Angel! Yes! Yes!" and pulled his dick out, releasing himself to me completely.

I could feel the goose bumps on his arms as he lay next to me. He trembled as I touched him. Then, he put his arms around me, holding me close to his heart and I drifted peacefully off to sleep as he kissed my lips goodnight.

And then came the drama!!!

Come visit me at
www.myspace.com/1koleblack

Printed in the United States
126330LV00005B/151/A